Louisa has clambered halfway down the ladder but stops to look across the alley at me with terror-filled eyes.

My mind races as I consider my options, none of them good. I can hide here in my room and hope the Alliance spy doesn't find me.

Or I can get out of this window somehow.

But how?

I look across the alley. I look down at the ground, nine floors below me.

Bravery is doing what you have to do.

Even when you're scared to death.

Once again, there is no thought. Just action.

So I brace myself.

And jump.

TOMORROW GIRLS

Behind the Gates

Run for Cover

With the Enemy

Set Me Free

TOMORROW GIRLS

GIRLS

Set Me Free

BY EVA GRAY

SCHOLASTIC INC.

New York   Toronto   London   Auckland
Sydney   Mexico City   New Delhi   Hong Kong

ISBN 978-0-545-31704-7

12 11 10 9 8 7 6 5 4 3 2   11 12 13 14 15 16/0

Printed in the U.S.A.   40
First printing, November 2011

Chapter 1

It's strange how everything you know about the world — and yourself — can change in a fraction of a second.

Just moments ago, I was being rescued from an Alliance prison where I was actually being brainwashed into becoming my own enemy.

Then I was in a van with my friends, hurtling toward the rest of our group. And I was given a piece of information that flipped everything upside down.

The Hornet is Madeleine Frye's mother.

The leader of the Resistance. My mom.

You see, I've always been ordinary. Ordinary Madeleine Frye. I was timid and cautious, a girl known mostly for her wild, curly hair . . . while the rest of me was tame.

But everything is different now.

Now I stand in an empty lot with my friends: Louisa, Rosie, Evelyn, Ryan, and Jonah. They are looking at the smoldering pile of crumbling brick and cinder block, which, Louisa told me, was once a car wash where they'd sought shelter. But now it's gone, as is the rest of our group: Drew and Alonso. My friends are, understandably, freaking out, but I can't focus on the implications of this new disaster yet.

Instead, all I can do is turn something over and over in my hands. It's a little alabaster box in the shape of a hornet's honeycomb hive. The box was given to me by the same person who changed my life by telling me about my mother's secret identity. The box is an answer, a question, a test. Small as it is, it seems to weigh a zillion pounds.

"Who do you think did this?" I hear Louisa asking Rosie, her voice taut with anxiety and fear. She gestures to the wreckage, her blue eyes wide. "The Alliance?"

Rosie shakes her head. Her silky black hair, loose from its gold band, swooshes back and forth. "No. The government. Look." She points, and Ryan gasps.

Sure enough, there is a small notice affixed to the fence that surrounds the lot. SCHEDULED FOR DEMOLITION is written in bold black letters at the top. FUTURE SITE OF CHICAGO WATER SANITIZING PLANT.

Evelyn's sharp, dark eyes fill with regret. I can tell, from the set of her mouth, how worried she is about Drew and Alonso — especially Alonso. They'd seemed to have formed a bond. "*How* did we not notice that before?" she asks, and I can tell she's beating herself up.

"You were preoccupied," I remind her. "Focused on more important matters, like the Phoenix Center."

Rosie nods at me, as if I'm making sense, but I'm not sure I am. My mind is doing this weird thing where it slams back and forth between clear and hazy.

Here's what's clear: several weeks ago, I went to a place called Country Manor School. I was posing as the sister of my best friend, Louisa, because my parents are both off fighting in the War (or so I thought) and *Louisa's*

3

parents thought this CMS place would be a safe and wonderful experience for Louisa and me. They were sorely mistaken.

As the War escalated beyond the gates of our cushy school, we found out that CMS was actually run by the enemy — the Alliance — and we so-called students were more like hostages. Louisa and I and our two roommates, Rosie and Evelyn, knew we had to get away. We escaped into the woods, where we met Drew, Alonso, and Ryan, who were from the CMS boys' school. Together, we began our journey to Chicago — where our families are — but on the way, I was kidnapped and brought to the Phoenix Center.

The Phoenix Center was a strange, dim place — a school unlike any I'd known. There were lie detectors in the classrooms and a complicated "spying game" we students had to play on one another at all times. But somehow I'd felt that I belonged there. The administration had made me feel worthy and important — a part of something significant — like I'd never really felt before. Except it had all been a lie.

4

My friends had rescued me from Phoenix, with the help of a guy named Ivan, who'd been posing as a Phoenix scout but was really a Resistance soldier. Ivan was the one who'd told me about my mother, and had given me the box.

Here's what's hazy: how I'm supposed to follow Ivan's directive to deliver this box to my mother when I have no idea where she is.

Up until a little while ago, I didn't even know *who* she is.

The Hornet, I've just learned, is the code name for the leader of the Resistance. The Resistance forces are working to put a stop to the evil Alliance, and even end the War. That this powerful person is my own mother is still mind-boggling.

I glance up from the box momentarily, and look over at Jonah. He was at Phoenix with me. When my friends came for me, I insisted that Jonah also come with us. I feel a huge sense of loyalty to him because when I first got to Phoenix, he saved my life. Good reason, right?

Jonah still hasn't made eye contact with anyone directly, and he's purposely standing off to the side. I think this is something you learn when you live in a gang-infested city, fighting for your life and wondering when you'll eat next. In the past, someone like Jonah would have frightened me, but right now, I just wish there was something I could do or say to make him feel safe with us.

Only none of *us* feels safe.

"What are we going to do?" Evelyn asks with rising panic. She's a worrier, and thinks conspiracies are behind everything. And as it turns out, she is often right. We'd grown close at CMS, and she was someone I found myself missing during quiet moments at the Phoenix Center.

"We had everything in that car wash," she continues, pacing back and forth, "our backpacks and tools and documents. And . . ." She pauses and looks up. "Helen and Drew and — and Alonso . . . Are they . . ." She trails off.

Helen? Who's Helen? I think. Curious as I am, I know that question will have to wait.

It's as if we all stop breathing at once as the same horrifying thought crosses our minds.

"Do you think they were . . . inside?" Louisa ventures, nervously tugging on the end of her blond ponytail. Tears threaten in her voice. Ryan reaches out and clumsily pats her arm.

I should hug her, be a good best friend. But I'm frozen in fear and confusion.

"No," Rosie says, quickly and decisively — ever the leader. "No, they definitely weren't. A bulldozer or a wrecking ball did this, and those aren't exactly things that can sneak up on you, right?"

Evelyn nods at Rosie, looking calmer. "When they heard the machines approaching, they would have run. Even with Drew's and Alonso's injuries, they would have been quick," she reasons out.

Drew's and Alonso's injuries? I think. What went on while my friends and I were separated? What have I missed?

"Do you think they're hiding nearby?" Ryan speaks up, his bright blue eyes troubled. I realize that, like Jonah, he's been quiet all this time. Maybe boys have a different way of dealing with worry than girls. They clam up.

We all look around at the silent, empty landscape. There's not a sound other than the wind. No one has to point out that if the others had been hiding, they would have come out already. Revealed themselves to us.

Rosie immediately whips out what looks to be a modified old cell phone. I can't begin to imagine where that came from, but this isn't the time to ask. She is punching the "talk" button and, walkie-talkie style, shouting into it for Drew or Alonso to answer her. Unfortunately, neither of them does.

"Out of range," sighs Ryan. "Or out of battery."

"So where did they *go*?" Louisa asks, wearily resting her head on Rosie's shoulder.

I feel a quick little stab of jealousy, which is silly at a time like this. But at CMS I'd been wary of Rosie, particularly because she and Louisa had grown so close. The kids at CMS were like Louisa: privileged, wealthy, special. Rosie was no exception. She'd bark out orders and everyone listened to her. I suppose it's a good thing we did, though, because when it comes to quick thinking and leadership, Rosie scores high marks. I think I'm a little jealous of that, too.

Jonah clears his throat, and everyone glances at him in surprise. His voice low and rough, he mutters, "Do you think they went home?"

Home. My heart squeezes. I haven't been home — to my real home — in ages, because I was living with Louisa's family before we left for CMS. I look around at everyone's faces. No one has been home in far too long. Especially Jonah, who'd been living on the streets before he was picked up and taken to Phoenix School.

"They wouldn't," Louisa sniffs, shaking her head. "We figured out that Alliance agents are posted at all of our houses. It wouldn't be safe for us, or our families."

At the word *families* I turn the honeycomb box over in my hands again, and, like Evelyn, I start pacing, too. I pace when I want to think better. The box, my mom, Alonso, Drew . . . everything is rattling around in my head.

Then I stop short of stepping into a sprawling smear of orange goop. It seems to be a loopy trail of something the consistency of toothpaste or old-fashioned cake frosting (I've never tasted real sugar frosting, but I'd read about it and seen it in old movies). As I step over the goop, I nearly trip over a can with an orange cap. It rolls away, rumbling across the lot.

"Hey, that's the can of Cheezy-Wizard we got when we stole all that food from the library," says Ryan. He sounds wistful. Ryan is the big eater of the group.

I'm studying the orange glop. I'm not sure what stolen food Ryan's talking about, but I do know this: *the orange mess is actually made up of letters.*

"Somebody wrote something with that Cheezy-Wizard!" I exclaim, my heart jumping.

The others, except Jonah, join me to take a look.

"Graffiti?" asks Jonah from where he stands at a distance. He pushes his unruly dark hair away from his eyes, which are a calm but intense green.

Back in the Phoenix School, Jonah told me that graffiti artists are usually members of violent street crews who mark their turf by painting their symbols and names all around the area they control, as warnings for other gangs to stay out: FANG TERRITORY — KEEP OUT; BLADES ONLY; DEATH TO THE DAGGERS; et cetera. I would guess that these tags are done with actual paint, not processed cheese spread. Which means . . .

"It's not graffiti," I say, my pulse pounding with hope. "I think it's a message. From our friends."

"She's right," says Rosie, and I find I'm glad to have her affirmation.

Louisa brightens, her blue eyes sparkling with relief. "Drew and Alonso and Helen must have used the Cheezy-Wizard to tell us something."

Everyone leans closer, squinting as we try to decipher the words.

It's more difficult than it sounds. The fact that Alonso or Drew or Helen — whoever she is — used a can of Cheezy-Wizard as a writing utensil makes the scribble pretty illegible. We are a generation who learned to type in pre-K, so even under the best of circumstances our handwriting skills are pretty primitive. The only real writing I ever did was in this little puzzle book my mom gave me when I was about seven. It was a blank journal that we used to create cryptograms and play word games. Well, my mom created them; the challenge was for me to solve them. She called them "mental calisthenics" designed to improve my thinking skills and my vocabulary. Which I could really rely on right now.

"It's a *W*," says Rosie. "Right? That first letter is a capital *W*."

"And that one's an *R*," says Louisa, pointing. "And I *think* that's a *G*."

"*W-R-G*?" I say out loud, frowning in confusion. "Is it some kind of code? An acronym?"

"You always think in codes," Louisa tells me with a smile, giving me a nudge, and for a split second, it feels like old times.

"Is the last letter a *Y*?" Ryan asks, crouching down to look.

12

"Yes," Evelyn says, walking a circle around the smear. "I'm pretty sure there's an *L* in there, too. So . . ."

"*W-R-G-L-Y*," I say, wracking my brain.

"Wait," Louisa says, her eyes lighting up. "It's *not* a code. It's just a word with a letter missing. It says *Wrigley!*"

"As in Wrigley Field?" I ask.

Wrigley Field is the baseball stadium that was once a Chicago landmark. It's a place I know well, since it's just a short L ride from my house. Or it was, back when both the field and the L trains were still operational. The stadium is closed now, condemned. Some say it's even haunted. Or inhabited by weird creatures. But I push those rumors out of my head.

"Yes, Wrigley Field," Evelyn chimes in, examining the writing. "It has to be. That's where we'll find our friends."

"Then let's go!" Ryan is already heading back to the stolen Phoenix van he hot-wired for my rescue. We follow him eagerly and we all pile in. I notice Jonah hesitate beside the sliding door.

13

"Come with us," I urge, thinking he's worried about wearing out his welcome.

He looks as though he wants to say something, but instead, he just climbs in and pulls the door shut behind him.

In the next second, Ryan is steering the vehicle out of the parking lot, leaving the remains of the car wash behind us and heading toward Wrigley Field . . . and whatever we will find there.

Chapter 2

In the van, I can tell something is still eating at Jonah. He chews his bottom lip and stares at his sneakers. Meanwhile, Ryan keeps his eyes on the road, Rosie is trying to reach Drew or Alonso on the walkie-talkie (in vain), and Evelyn and Louisa sit in silence. Louisa keeps one arm looped through mine, as if that will somehow keep me in place from now on. And somehow, it does make me feel safer.

"What's wrong?" I ask Jonah, still gripping the honeycomb in my clammy palm. I know it's hard for him to open up, so I give his shoulder an encouraging pat, and then he begins to talk.

"When I lived on the streets," he explains, "even the worst thugs stayed away from Wrigley Field. They said there were mutants there. Freaks. Scary ones."

I stare at him. Jonah's afraid of something? I wouldn't have expected that.

"Mutants?" says Louisa fearfully.

"Calm down," Rosie says, glancing back at us. "If Jonah knows about these rumors, then I'm sure Helen does, too. Those *rumors* are probably exactly why she decided she, Drew, and Alonso should hide out at Wrigley Field." She says this in that commanding and confident voice she's so good at. "The cops never go there because of those stories, and I'm pretty sure the Alliance wouldn't chance it, either."

So Helen was a street kid, too, I muse. I want to ask more about her, but then Ryan speaks up.

"Let's just say there are mutants," he says, taking a left onto North Racine. "What exactly are we talking about here? Webbed feet? Eyes in the backs of their heads?"

You'd think the daughter of the Hornet, one of the most important women in the country, wouldn't get a sinking feeling in her stomach at the mention of webbed feet. But suddenly I'm petrified. Jonah doesn't look convinced, either. I guess I don't blame him. He doesn't even know Drew or Alonso or Helen, so why would he risk stumbling upon mutants to help strangers?

Then again, I was a stranger and he helped me.

"Maybe we should rethink this," I say, and Louisa nods at me. "I mean, I'm all for finding the others, but shouldn't we formulate some kind of mutant defense plan first?"

"Okay, this is insane," says Evelyn, rolling her eyes. She looks right at me. "Maddie, don't tell me you actually think there's a band of violent humanoids living at Wrigley Field. Seriously? Do you really believe that?"

I'm stunned. "You *don't?*" I ask. "You're always insisting that sinister stuff is lurking behind the shadows."

"I know," Evelyn admits, and gives me a funny smile — it's sheepish, mixed with a little bit of pride.

17

"And I do still believe that the Alliance is more powerful than we realize, that they're likely slipping subliminal messages into music lyrics and secretly poisoning our air supply." She shrugs. "But the whole mutant thing just sounds silly to me."

Louisa cocks her head at Evelyn. "So . . . you think deadly mutants are silly, but a *music* threat makes perfect sense to you?"

"I'm just saying," says Evelyn, "we've got enough scary reality to worry about, so why waste time on fairy tales?"

She's got a point. I begin to relax a little.

"And besides," says Rosie, "let's say, for argument's sake, there *are* mutants living in Wrigley. We aren't just going to let Alonso, Drew, and Helen face them alone, are we? I mean, if we don't have their backs, who will?"

I nod. I *want* to be brave. I figure going ahead with this plan is a good start.

As we head the few miles up North Racine Avenue, I see a boarded-up old bookstore, out of use forever. It reminds me of Phoenix School. Since the building was formerly a public library, there were plenty of books in storage. My chore was to burn them as a symbol of "heralding in a new world order, getting rid of the dangerous old ideas." But those books hadn't felt dangerous to me. They'd felt important. On my ultralightweight titanium e-reader (long since abandoned at CMS), you'd hit "delete" when you finished a story and it all just disappeared. But these leather-bound books had a real sense of permanence about them. I picture the books and their titles in my mind: *Tom Sawyer*, *The Hunger Games*, *Little Women*, *The Odyssey* . . . Gone now, because of me.

Ryan stops to let a car go ahead of him. It's an older model, an electronic-petroleum hybrid. The advertisement on the side door is a splashy red one for Jumpy Juice, a pomegranate-flavored energy drink. According to the ad, not only does the beverage effect a chemical reaction in the brain to provide forty-eight hours of pure vigor but it can also, oddly enough, make your hair more manageable.

I've never tasted a pomegranate, but I'm pretty sure Jumpy Juice isn't worth the risk. And my unmanageable hair is the least of my problems right now.

Not too long ago, Louisa and I would have laughed

19

about that ad, but things are so different now. I look at Louisa, and I wonder if she's remembering how things were tense between us before I was taken. I'm also wondering how I'll ever find my mom in what seems like an increasingly big and dangerous Chicago . . . if she's even *in* Chicago at all.

Trying to get my mind off my mother, I turn to Louisa. "So . . . who's Helen?" I finally ask.

All talking over one another, Rosie, Ryan, Louisa, and Evelyn explain that Helen was a runaway from Phoenix — a "flier," we'd called those who'd broken out — and she, as well as her brother, Troy, had stumbled upon the group not long after I'd been taken. Helen was wild and tough, but she'd proven helpful — she was the one who'd given my friends the inside knowledge of Phoenix's rules so that they could infiltrate the school and get to me. I feel a rush of gratitude toward this girl I've never met.

"So in some ways it's thanks to Helen that I'm even here with all of you again," I muse out loud, still trying to come to grips with everything that's happened.

"And to Ivan," Rosie points out from the passenger seat. Ivan is the boyfriend of Rosie's sister, Wren. I know she's worrying about him — and Wren, too. According to Ivan, Wren is stationed with the Hornet — my mom. And I know Rosie is as desperate to find her sister as I am to find my mother.

"And all of you," I add, looking from Louisa to Evelyn and feeling a tightening in my throat. "And you," I add, turning to Jonah.

"Maddie, you said something about Jonah saving your life at Phoenix," Evelyn speaks up. "What happened?"

Jonah's looking straight ahead. He seems embarrassed, but I think maybe if I tell my friends about his heroic act, he'll feel more comfortable with us.

"It was the first night I was there," I say. "After they grabbed me from the mall parking lot."

"Right," says Rosie, softly. "We remember that part."

"I was so scared," I tell them, recalling the heart-pounding terror, the sense of dread and bewilderment as the van drove through the darkness and I was powerless to stop it. "More scared than I'd ever been in my life." I hesitate, unable to speak for a moment. Louisa squeezes my elbow.

I'm surprised to hear Jonah pick up the story. "I saw Maddie when they first brought her in," he says quietly but evenly. "She didn't have the look."

"What look?" Ryan asks.

"The look of a street kid. That crazy, desperate look in the eyes that comes from being afraid and forgotten."

I shiver; was that how Jonah had looked when the Alliance found him on the street and dragged him into the Phoenix School?

I find my voice again and continue. "The Superior showed me around the school. Her name was Miss Castle."

Jonah shudders at the mention of her name.

"I remember her," says Rosie in a voice of dread.

"Me, too," says Evelyn. "She's that old lady who Ivan said could maim you with her knitting needles."

"It was kill you with her pinkie," Louisa clarifies.

I twist the honeycomb in my hands again. "Miss Castle made it sound like some cool museum tour, like at

22

the end I could buy souvenirs or something. Then I noticed this older girl following us — Brianna, her name was — and she kept giving me these really mean, cold looks."

"Brianna was on the streets a long time," says Jonah. "By the time she got to Phoenix, she wasn't all there in the head. The Alliance recognized that right off, which is why they were training her in the most dangerous stuff."

"Like what?" asks Ryan from behind the wheel, sounding as though he'd rather not know the answer.

"Explosives. She spent a lot of time in the pyrotechnics lab." Jonah actually smiles, but there is no humor in it. "Otherwise known as the Boom Room."

My friends are looking a little pale now, I guess because they're really beginning to understand the true nature of the Phoenix Center. They'd been on the inside, but only briefly.

Jonah continues. "I noticed Brianna shadowing Maddie when the Superior was showing her the kitchen. I was there helping unload the daily three-o'clock food delivery. When I saw Brianna following Maddie, it was like I snapped out of my haze for a second. I decided to follow them."

I give him a look of gratitude. "The last stop on the tour was the boiler room," I say, "with those roaring fires. I actually found myself thinking that it might be nice to have such a warm place to be on a cold night." I shake my head, remembering the burning books. "Brianna followed me along the upper catwalk." Even with the fires blazing I could feel my blood chilling.

The van rocks gently as Ryan takes a corner, and I take a breath.

"Right then, Miss Castle got a call on her communication device. She told me to wait for her. The minute she was gone, Brianna came up behind me. She grabbed me by the shoulders and kept shaking me, pushing me closer and closer to the railing of the catwalk." I can feel the heat of the flames on the back of my neck even now.

Louisa gasps. Rosie's eyes are huge. Evelyn is shaking her head in horror.

"And then Jonah was there and he was talking to Brianna, very quietly, and very, very calmly."

"Calmly?" says Ryan, impressed. "I would have been freaking out!"

"I *was* freaking out," I assure him. "But Jonah kept it together. He said things like, 'You don't want to do this, Brianna. You know you don't want to get in more trouble.'"

I'm remembering the easy, relaxed cadence of his words. Underneath them there was also this firmness that left no room for argument. Luckily, Brianna had recognized that, too.

Evelyn is wringing her hands, breathless with the suspense of it. "What happened?"

"Well, she's *here*," Rosie points out, "so I'm thinking his little pep talk was successful."

I nod. "Brianna just let go of me," I say, feeling the shock and relief all over again. "She just let go and backed away. Then she took off running."

"Did you go after her?" Louisa asks Jonah.

"Well . . ." Jonah shoots me a look. "I couldn't."

25

"Why not?" Louisa demands to know.

"Because he had his hands full," I explain, blushing. "See, after Brianna let go of me, I kind of, well, um . . ."

"She fainted," says Jonah, simply.

"Yeah, I fainted. And I guess Jonah caught me."

"Good thing," quips Ryan, "considering you were hovering above an enormous fiery pit at the time."

"Miss Castle came back and told me to bring her to the medical facility," says Jonah.

This was where things grew dim and fuzzy for me. So I listen intently as Jonah describes how he helped me down the rickety steps of the catwalk, and through the corridors to the infirmary. He explains that two nurses in Phoenix-issue lab coats instructed him to place me on a cot. He offered to stay with me, but they said absolutely not, that this was a restricted zone, patients only.

"So I left, but I hid and watched them," Jonah tells us. "I was hoping they wouldn't do it, but they did."

"Do what?" Louisa asks.

I bite my lip, looking at him nervously. This part of the story is news to me. My heart bangs against my ribs and I grip the honeycomb so hard I worry I'll break it.

"Phoenix uses all different methods of mind control," he says, "which they help along by feeding us food laced with low doses of slow-acting drugs."

"How do you know this?" Evelyn asks, looking both suspicious and deeply curious.

"It's pretty obvious," says Jonah, clearly growing more comfortable. "No one's ever said it out loud, but since they don't give us pills or anything, the smarter ones have figured out that it's the food that's doing it."

"The NutriCorp food we found," says Rosie. "Now it all makes sense."

"And you can't just *not* eat," says Ryan.

"But Maddie was only at Phoenix for three days," Rosie points out. "And I've seen her eat. She's not exactly a chowhound . . . like some people I know." She jabs Ryan in the side.

"It's true," I say, frowning. "And if the drugs in the food are slow-acting, how did I get so dopey so quickly?"

Jonah is about to answer but is cut off by the shriek of rubber skidding on cement. Ryan has slammed on the van's brakes to avoid hitting a stray dog that has appeared in the street. My first instinct is to hop out of the van and help the animal, but even as I am reaching for the door, Jonah's hand clamps down on my wrist to stop me. In the next second, I understand why: four more mutts have joined the one in the street. They are all lean with dull, matted coats and wild eyes. They stand there, like a canine blockade, panting and pawing the asphalt.

"Ooh, look," says Ryan in a deadpan tone. "Fluffy and Rover want to play."

One of the dogs, a German shepherd–pit bull mix I think, actually sits up on his hind legs and howls at the van before they all scamper off together into an alley on the opposite side of the street. I watch them go, wondering if they ever had homes, and feeling an odd empathy toward them.

Ryan drives on, and Jonah continues.

"I watched one nurse roll up your sleeve," he tells me, his big eyes serious. "The other one was at the counter with her back to me but I could tell she was preparing something. I saw that they were talking but I couldn't hear them."

"I could," I blurt out, only realizing it now. "I mean, I think I could."

"But you were unconscious," Evelyn points out.

"I was," I tell her. "At first. But then I started to come out of it. It was like waking up from a really deep sleep, the kind where you can't tell if you're dreaming. I remember hearing voices. They seemed muffled and I could only make out maybe every other word." I am struggling to recall the sounds and sensations, and that's when the memory hits me.

"It hurt!" I exclaim, my hand going instinctively to my left arm. "I remember feeling it! The nurse was preparing a hypodermic needle!"

"Yep," says Jonah. "That's when I knew that they had big plans for you. They weren't gonna just wait around

29

for those 'special spices' in their soy burgers to take effect on Madeleine Frye." He lets out a long rush of breath.

Now I understand why my mind's been rolling back and forth like it has. The drugs are still wearing off. I'm filled with disgust. The thought of chemicals in my body makes me sick.

"That is twisted and evil," Rosie says, curling her hands into fists.

"I guess the stab of that needle is what brought me out of my daze," I say. "But I didn't cry out. I didn't even flinch. I was so afraid of what they would do to me if they knew I was awake that I just stayed perfectly still and kept my eyes closed."

"So you *did* hear what they were saying," Ryan prompts. "What were they talking about?"

I squeeze my eyes shut and try to remember. "Something about a storm, maybe?"

"So they were talking about the weather," sighs Evelyn, disappointed. "Everyone does that."

The weather *is* a common topic of conversation since it's so unpredictable these days. The week before we went to CMS there was a windstorm that took out windows and downed power lines all over Chicago. The next day it was nearly ninety degrees and the day after that it went down to almost freezing.

I push my thoughts backward, struggling to hear the echo of the nurses' conversation. "They were also talking about something . . . irresistible," I report.

"Irresistible?" says Ryan. "You mean like choco-soy cupcakes?"

I shake my head, wishing I could chase down the memory. Evelyn gives me a reassuring look, and I hope I will remember when I need to.

We can see the stadium in the distance now. The van grows quiet as we make our final approach. Hopefully Drew and Alonso and Helen are there.

And hopefully, the mutants aren't.

Ryan guides the van to the curb in front of Wrigley Field. We climb out and stare silently at the gigantic, crumbling stadium looming above us like some haunted castle. At one time, or so my parents had told me, the big red sign was a proud symbol of our city. Now the once-brilliant red has faded to a sickly pinkish color, and most of the letters are missing

"Home . . . o . . . hi . . . ago . . . ubs," reads Ryan.

"I think it's supposed to say, home of Chicago Cubs," says Evelyn. "The sign used to light up."

"Must have been cool," says Rosie.

"I remember baseball," says Ryan. There is sadness in his eyes as he absently punches his right hand into his left palm, as though wearing an imaginary baseball mitt. "My dad kept all his old equipment from when he was a kid, and we used to play catch in the backyard. Mom would bring us out lemonade and watch."

We take one more wistful look at the sign before we silently summon the courage to enter beneath it.

We pass single file through the least-rusted turnstile and find ourselves in a broad, shadowy corridor. The walls and floor are made of cement, which creates a sort of echo-chamber effect.

And unfortunately, what's echoing through it right now is the sound of footsteps.

Chapter 3

The sound ricochets off the cold gray walls, getting closer by the second. The footsteps are slow, heavy, and weirdly offbeat. The rhythm starts with a *thud*, and ends with a *thump*, with this eerie, elongated scraping sound in between. *Thud-draaaaggg-thump-clunk . . . thud-draaaaggg-thump-clunk . . .*

I hold my breath. Louisa grabs my hand.

"He's getting closer," Rosie whispers.

"Whatever 'he' is," gulps Evelyn. She looks like she's rethinking her opinions on the mutants.

Now the footsteps stop entirely, and the echo ripples in the silence. And then, the voice.

The voice asks, "Who's there?"

Evelyn and I nearly jump out of our skins. Louisa squeezes my hand so hard I feel my knuckles crack. Rosie, though, squares her shoulders and says in a courageous tone, "Show yourself first."

There is a moment of hesitation that seems to last a lifetime, and then there is another short series of *thud*s and *drag*s, and then there he is.

He's not a mutant. He's just a normal guy, maybe about Ivan's age: eighteen or so. Like Ivan, he's well built and lean, but I notice that he's using a cane, which explains the clunking sound. It's not an actual cane he's leaning on, but a baseball bat. His hair is a little scraggly and his hazel eyes are wary, but not menacing.

"What's the password?" the guy demands.

Obviously, we have no idea.

"Listen," says Ryan, his voice cracking only a little. "We have reason to believe our friends are here. If you can tell us where they are, we'll get out of your way."

And that's when I hear the shouting — two familiar,

muffled voices calling for help. *Drew and Alonso.* I can tell Rosie hears it, too. She shoots a quick look at Louisa, who turns and sends the silent look to me. Maybe our adventure has turned us into mind readers or maybe it's just common sense, but I know what they're thinking: *This guy walks in slow motion. We can outrun him and get to our friends.*

Of course, if he's armed, the mad dash they're contemplating will be the worst idea in history. I tamp down every rational thought in my brain. They're willing; I should be, too.

Rosie gives us a signal with her eyes, and in the next second, she, Louisa, and I are running. We bolt right past the guy, catching him completely off guard. I can't be sure if the others have heard the shouting, too, or if they just follow us in a show of blind trust, but Evelyn, Ryan, and Jonah take off a split second after we do.

We get to the end of the corridor and thunder down a short flight of cement steps. There, tied to each other, back-to-back, are Drew and Alonso.

Fortunately, they appear to be unhurt. Alonso's brown eyes show his gratitude as Rosie and Evelyn immediately set about untying them.

"Maddie!" shouts Drew. "You're all right!" As soon as he's free, he throws his arms around me in a brotherly hug, nearly knocking his wire-rimmed glasses off his face.

"I guess the plan at the Phoenix worked out okay?" Alonso asks, grinning at me.

I nod, still feeling a little numb. I'm grateful when Evelyn jumps in and explains to Drew and Alonso about Ivan, our escape, and the revelation that my mom is the Hornet. Drew and Alonso look stunned and impressed — especially Drew. He's looking at me as if with new eyes.

"I never knew," I tell them, feeling a mix of conflicting emotions. "But are you guys all right?" I ask, wanting to change the subject for the moment.

"We're fine," says Alonso. "That guy with the bat's actually pretty decent. After he tied us up, he looked at both our injuries. He wrapped my knee and re-bandaged Drew's shoulder."

So these were the injuries Evelyn mentioned. I remember that Drew tried to stop my kidnappers by slamming his shoulder into the car door. He tried to save me. First Drew, then Jonah. I guess chivalry isn't dead after all. I give Drew a smile of thanks. Secretly, though, I don't like the fact that when it comes to being a damsel in distress, I would be considered a repeat offender. I find myself wishing I could be as self-reliant as Evelyn, or as brave as Louisa, or as in control as Rosie.

Or as All of the Above as my mother.

"So, wait," says Ryan. "If this guy is such a good sport, why'd he, you know, *tie you up*?"

"He said he needed to be sure our story checked out and we weren't gang members," Alonso explains. "We told him you'd probably be coming here and you'd vouch for us."

"You knew we'd be coming?" Evelyn asks, looking at Alonso with a kind of openness and relief that makes me realize she might . . . like him. A lot. And Alonso nods at Evelyn, looking at her in the same way. *Hmm.*

37

For a second, I glance at Jonah, and my heart somersaults.

"Hey," says Drew with a slow smile, his dark eyes crinkling up. "Which one of you figured out the Cheezy-Wizard clue?"

"Louisa did," says Rosie proudly, and Louisa turns pink as Drew and Alonso thank her.

Evelyn is thrilled to see that Drew and Alonso remembered to bring along our backpacks when they fled the car wash, so what meager supplies and information we had is still safe. Louisa glances around, frowning.

"Wait. Where's Helen?" she asks.

"She came with us as far as the stadium," Drew explains. "But she was worried about her brother, Troy."

"She said she was going to try to find him," says Alonso. "She had to make sure he was all right."

I notice Rosie nodding, because she totally gets that. She's been looking for her sister for years.

"Helen asked us to tell all of you good-bye," says Alonso. "And good luck."

Louisa smiles. "Maybe we'll run into her again some-time. And Troy, too."

That's Louisa. Always finding the bright side of things, always hoping for the best.

"Run *into*?" Rosie asks, grinning wickedly. "That's a nice way to put it. Don't you remember the first time we 'ran into' them? When they had me in a headlock?"

Louisa laughs. "Okay, okay. Good point."

At that same moment, Alonso and Drew seem to notice Jonah for the first time. They raise their eyebrows at him, this new boy in their midst, and Jonah looks down again, sticking his hands in his pockets. I'm starting to introduce him when we hear the *thud-draaaaggg-thump-clunk* sound. The guy with the bat is approaching us. But this time his expression is no longer one of mis-trust. He actually seems relieved.

"I should have known you guys were telling the truth," he tells Drew and Alonso. "You didn't look gang-affiliated."

Then, for some reason, he looks at me. His expres-sion is focused and intent, as though he's trying to place where he knows me from. But I've never seen him before.

"We're not," Rosie says stonily. "But before we tell you who *we* are . . . why don't you tell us?"

At first, he looks a little taken aback at being challenged by a thirteen-year-old girl. Then he answers her. "I'm Dizzy," he says simply. "I live here."

We each go around and give our first names only. We say nothing about where we've come from or why. You can't be too careful. Jonah barely mutters his name. When I say "Maddie," Dizzy looks at me with a jolt of recognition. I don't think it's my name he recognizes, though.

Evelyn is the last one to speak. She says her name, then narrows her eyes at Dizzy. "So your name is really *Dizzy?*" she asks him incredulously.

"It's a nickname," he explains. "My real name is Dean, but a long time ago there was this great baseball player — a pitcher for the Cubs — who went by the nickname Dizzy Dean. I figured since I'm living in the stadium he once called home, it was kind of a nice tribute."

"I'm just glad you're not some three-headed mutant, with spikes growing out of your spine," says Ryan.

"Oh, that guy . . ." Dizzy jerks his thumb toward the exit. "He lives over at Union Stock Yard. We occasionally meet for lunch, though."

Something about the chuckle just under his words makes me realize.

"You started the rumors!" I exclaim. "You made up all that mutant stuff yourself!"

Dizzy answers with a grin that makes him look as boyish as Ryan. "I can't take all the credit," he confesses. "Those crazy legends have been floating around since the day they closed the stadium. Let's just say I made a point of perpetuating them and, while I was at it, embellishing them a bit."

"Just to keep people out?" says Louisa. "For privacy?"

"It's more than privacy, isn't it?" Rosie challenges him again. "You're hiding out for another reason."

Dizzy swallows, and looks at each of us carefully. Then he lets out a breath and says, "I'm a Resistance soldier." There's a beat of silence and I feel a wave of, well, dizziness sweep over me. Dizzy glances away, then clarifies, "Well, a former Resistance soldier, at any rate."

"Former?" Evelyn's on alert now. "Are you a traitor?" she demands. "A double agent?" Her hands curl into fists and she takes a step forward.

Surprisingly, when Rosie reaches out to pull Evelyn back, the gesture is friendly, not bossy, like I would have expected from Rosie. This is weird because back at CMS these two bickered constantly.

"Relax. He's obviously no longer active because of his injury." Rosie turns back to the guy. "Right? You were injured in the line of duty, fighting for the Resistance."

"That is correct." The guy shifts on his wounded leg, then looks pointedly at me. "Which is why I know your mother."

The floor seems to drop out from under me. I can only gawk at him, speechless. Is this a trap or a trick? What can I say?

"Why should I believe you?" I manage to get out.

Dizzy eyes me steadily. "You look just like her," he says, as a sort of answer. "You are the daughter of Lorraine Frye, are you not?" he asks. "Or, as we call her, the Hornet."

Lorraine. My mother's name. I hadn't thought of it in so long. And I know I do look like my mom — we have the same fair skin and curly hair. People would tell us all the time. I don't think Dizzy is lying.

"I can't believe your mom is the *Hornet*," Drew says, sounding stunned.

"I'm just as shocked as you," I tell him. My mind is reeling and I can feel all my friends watching me as I look back at Dizzy. "Yes, I am her daughter," I say.

Dizzy nods back at me. "I was sure," he says softly. "I didn't know her well. I don't even know where she is stationed now. But it was an honor to serve under her. She's a brave and brilliant woman."

I want to ask Dizzy so much more — what exactly my mom was doing as the Hornet, if he knows anything about my dad . . . But I hold my tongue. I'm still not entirely sure I can trust him.

Rosie seems to read my mind. "So if you're really in the Resistance," she says, and there's still a challenge in her voice, "do you know someone named Ivan?"

Dizzy smiles. "Of course. Ivan Franks. We graduated from boot camp together and entered the main ranks of the Resistance. He's a heck of a soldier. Last I heard, he was stationed as a spy at the Phoenix Center. And his girlfriend, Wren Chavez, is with the Hornet — wherever that might be."

Rosie lets out a gasp at her sister's name. The rest of us exchange glances. We all seem to silently agree that Dizzy is legit. Which means he really *knows my mom*.

"So how did you end up here?" Jonah asks Dizzy.

Dizzy's smile fades. "Several months back, I was part of a reconnaissance unit up near the Canadian border. We heard there were the beginnings of an Alliance threat in the area. It was supposed to be an easy assignment, which it was. Until I had a little run-in with a grenade."

I lower my eyes and study my fingernails. The others are quiet, too.

"The Alliance soldier who threw it was about my age; I guess he got separated from his patrol squad, and when he saw me and my team, he panicked. Anyway, my buddies patched me up as best they could and got me back to Chicago, but a hospital was out of the question. We have to fly under the radar. I got the idea of taking up residence in this place. People already gave it a wide berth — even the cops and the Alliance tended to steer clear of it. All I had to do was keep the rumors afloat."

Louisa glances around, taking in the enormity of the old stadium. "You must get lonely."

"A little. Although, lately, I've been receiving visitors."

"Visitors?" Louisa echoes.

"It started by accident, actually. It was during one of those really intense electrical storms. A couple of street kids ducked in here looking for shelter. When we ran into each other, well, it's hard to say who was more scared,

45

me or them. I thought they were sent by the authorities to take me in; they were expecting the three-headed guy with the spikes. It took some very cautious negotiating, but we worked out a deal. A barter arrangement."

"Barter?" says Evelyn. "You mean like trade?"

"Exactly," says Dizzy. "They've got it tough out there. I, on the other hand, am living in the lap of luxury. I even was able to get the electricity in this place up and running."

"Where did you learn how to do that?" I ask.

"The Resistance doesn't just train us for combat; they educate us in all different areas of practical skills. Which is how I was also able to tap into one of the water mains the public works department must have forgotten about."

"So you let these street kids come here during storms and when they need medical attention," says Rosie. "What do they do for you?"

"They bring me food, when they can find it. The concession stands have freezers, so I can store things for a long time. They also do their part to keep the mutant rumors circulating, thus ensuring my continued privacy.

It's a pretty exclusive guest list. I have to be really selective about the kids I deal with. No one even remotely affiliated with the gangs is welcome. But the kids I've gotten to know and trust can let their friends in on the deal. They've got to give the password before I let them in."

"And when Drew and Alonso showed up," Evelyn says, putting it all together, "they didn't know the password, so you tied them up."

"I'm sorry about that," says Dizzy. "I kind of figured they were good kids, but you can never be too careful."

"Speaking of being careful," says Ryan, "we left our van nearby. What if the scouts see it and figure out where we are?"

Dizzy shakes his head. "Wouldn't worry about that if I were you."

"Why not?"

"In this neighborhood? I can pretty much guarantee the off-gridders and gangs are already dismantling it piece by piece."

Ryan looks a little sad about that. He liked having wheels, I guess.

Now Dizzy is looking at us more closely. We must look pretty bedraggled because he says, "Do you guys want to take showers?"

At this, everyone's faces brighten. I was able to shower at the Phoenix School, but now I just want to scrub every memory of that place off me. And I'm sure the others haven't had a chance to shower in ages.

"Oh, please tell me this isn't just some cruel joke," says Louisa, with longing in her voice.

"Nope," Dizzy says. "The water's even hot. There's also a small supply of soap and shampoo. And I've got clean towels. Well, clean enough, anyway."

"Clean enough is more than clean enough for me," says Alonso, running his hands through his wavy dark hair.

So Dizzy tells us the way to the locker rooms, and my friends take off at a run. I linger for a moment, wanting to ask Dizzy what else he might know about my mom, but then Louisa tugs my arm, and I follow her.

Chapter 4

The girls take the home team locker room; the boys take the visitors'.

The shower is heaven. The water pressure is pretty bad, and Dizzy's use of the word *hot* turns out to be relative. But *warm* still feels pretty darn good. I use small amounts of soap and shampoo, and relish the feeling of massaging my scalp and scrubbing my skin.

I step out into the locker room, wrapped in a towel. My friends are already dressed and I can't help myself — I crack up.

"What?" asks Rosie in a mock-insulted tone. "You disapprove of our wardrobe choices?" She struts from one end of the locker room to the other, like the supermodels that walked the catwalks when people still indulged in what they called "high fashion."

"Oh, I think you all look stunning!" I tell them.

"Good," says Louisa. "Because we've got a matching outfit for you."

The outfit, of course, is really an old Chicago Cubs uniform, and since they were made for grown men to wear, they are absolutely huge on us.

"The stripes are so flattering on you!" croons Evelyn, as I button up the front of the gigantic jersey they've found for me. "Honestly, darling, and that big number on the back is just so chic."

"And don't forget the hat!" says Louisa, plopping a blue cloth cap with a red "C" logo onto my damp hair. "Accessories are so important this season."

"And by that she means *baseball* season," giggles Rosie.

Thankfully, the enormous pants come with belts, so we manage to get them to stay up. We also dig up some clean pairs of socks and lace up our battered sneakers. Then I reach into the pocket of my old pants and take out the honeycomb, slipping it into my new pocket.

Once we're dressed, we stand in front of the locker room mirror, ignoring the huge lightning bolt–shaped crack that runs through it. At first, we can't stop giggling, but after a few minutes, we all grow serious. It's been a while since we've been able to linger in front of a mirror, even a broken one.

I wonder if my friends are thinking the same thing I am.

I look so different.

But not just different like you look when you get a new haircut, or when you've grown a quarter inch.

No.

My eyes have changed in a way that's hard to describe. There's more knowledge behind them. A deeper understanding of things.

And there's some fear in there, too. I won't deny it.

But there's also a distinct glimmer of hope.

"Look at us," whispers Louisa, her eyes meeting mine in the mirror. "We look like . . ."

"Idiots?" jokes Evelyn, tugging on the baggy sleeve of her bright blue jersey.

"Well, yes," Louisa agrees, smiling. "But also . . ."

"A team," I finish for her.

"We are a team," Evelyn says thoughtfully. "Even though we sure didn't start out that way."

"I know," Rosie says in a soft voice that almost doesn't sound like her. "Look . . . I'm sorry for how I may have . . . come off at first. At CMS."

"Same here," Louisa says, biting her lip and fiddling with her too-long sleeves. She's looking right at me as she says, "It was hard to adjust."

"We were all strangers to each other," Evelyn points out, tying her dark braids back into a ponytail. "Except for Louisa and Maddie, of course."

"But I was more than a stranger," I hear myself saying. "I was a full-on outsider. I mean, I wasn't even using my real name." I swallow hard, not wanting to say this next part, but knowing it needs to be said. Sensing my

52

apprehension, Evelyn reaches over and squeezes my hand for encouragement.

"I was jealous," I confess, looking at each of them. "I was jealous that you all came from wealthy families, with powerful, important parents."

"Well, as it happens, your parents are probably the most important of them all," Rosie points out.

I take this in for a moment, not sure I even believe it yet. And where does my dad fit into the Resistance? "But I didn't know that then," I finally reply. "And the thing I was most worried about was that I was . . . I was going to lose my best friend."

I turn to Louisa, and I'm not at all ashamed that there are tears in my eyes. "The other girls at CMS were more like you than I was — they had the same kind of upbringing, and they were going to grow up and have the same experiences as you. I was just . . . scared you were going to get bored of having such an ordinary friend like me." It feels good to get this truth out there.

Louisa doesn't hesitate. She throws her arms around

me and hugs me as hard as she can. "I'm sorry if I was acting like that," she says in a trembling voice. "I never meant to." I hug her back, hard.

"And believe me, Maddie," says Rosie once Louisa and I have pulled apart, "There is nothing ordinary about you."

I smile at her, feeling a lump in my throat.

"We were all outsiders when you think about it," says Evelyn.

"I realize that now," I say. "And the reason we've gotten this far is because of all the things we *didn't* have in common. Like, maybe we each have a quality that helps us through any crazy situation we might encounter."

"You don't know the half of it," sighs Rosie. "Wait until you hear what went down while you were at the Phoenix School."

Louisa, in her matter-of-fact way, proceeds to tell me everything from how she tended Drew's wound to their dangerous trek through the Settlement Lands. Then Evelyn relays how she found out where I was by hacking into a computer, and the intensive one-day training session led by the elusive Helen.

I'm about to ask Evelyn about Alonso — just to see if she might blush — but then we all hear a voice from the locker room entrance. It's Ryan.

And he's shouting, "Dinner!"

We follow Ryan to what used to be one of Wrigley's many concession stands.

"I'm starved," says Louisa, speaking for all of us. "What's on the menu?"

Ryan is beaming. "This is a ballpark! There are peanuts by the ton. And ballpark franks! Which, of course, are just regular soydogs. But somehow, they taste better when you eat them at a stadium."

Soydogs sound fine to me. Better than fine.

Dizzy, our host, is manning the concession stand. I feel wildly grateful to him as he passes each of us plump, steaming soydogs piled high with artificially flavored relish and sauerkraut. We sit down on some bleachers and we all dig in. My dog is warm and delicious, and tastes somehow . . . like tradition.

The others seem to be enjoying theirs just as much.

Even Jonah is grinning as he alternates between bites of his soydog and munches on a handful of peanuts.

As Dizzy goes off to get us waters, I take a deep breath and face my friends. Now that we've had a chance to catch our breaths, it's time for us to tackle what's been weighing on me ever since we left Phoenix.

I withdraw the honeycomb box from my pocket.

"What is *that*?" Alonso asks, swallowing a mouthful of soydog as his eyes light up with curiosity.

I quickly explain to him and Drew about Ivan instructing me to give the box to my mother. "If only I knew where she was," I finish.

"But Ivan didn't say," Evelyn begins, her expression thoughtful, "that we shouldn't *open* the box, right?"

I look at Evelyn, feeling a flutter of excitement.

"So maybe there's something inside," Jonah suggests quietly, "that will give us a clue as to where Maddie's mother is."

His voice seems tentative. Not because he doesn't think his suggestion is worthwhile (because it is) but because I think he's still feeling like an outsider. Obviously, I'm not the only one who notices.

I watch as Ryan pointedly offers Jonah a high five. "Excellent idea, dude," he says, grinning. "Good thing you came with us."

Jonah returns the hand smack, but remains somber. I want to give Ryan a hug for being so welcoming, but we've got to focus on the task at hand.

"So . . . I guess we should open it?" I say.

Rosie nods decisively. "We should."

By now, everyone has finished their soydogs and peanuts and has gathered closer to watch.

My heart pounding, I give the box a gentle twist, but nothing happens. Of course. That would be too easy.

"There's no lock on it, is there?" Ryan asks, leaning close to look in. "Or a keyhole?"

I shake my head, feeling frustrated. "I don't think so." For a moment I wonder if we could use Dizzy's bat to smash the box open, but I reject that idea immediately; doing that could destroy whatever's inside.

Slowly, I run my fingers over the rippled surface. The honeycomb pattern is a series of small, cuplike indentations, just large enough to fit the tip of my finger into.

"If there's no lock," I mutter, "then there's got to be another way to open it. Like maybe . . . a combination."

"Yes," says Louisa, sitting up straight. "A code! Didn't you say your mom was always into codes? That's where you get it from."

I nod, trying to concentrate. My locker at my old school had one of those keypads where you punch in a series of numbers, and for the first three weeks of eighth grade, I kept forgetting the combination they assigned to me. Then my mom spoke to the principal, and they allowed me to make up my own code, so it would be easier to remember. I felt silly, because none of the other kids needed to do that. But my mom explained that some people's minds were just better with words and letters than with numbers. When we switched the combination to a word of my choosing, I never forgot it again.

I'm staring at the box as though waiting for it to shout out the code for me, and I absently begin to count the holes that make up the honeycomb pattern.

"Twenty-six," I say aloud. "Twenty-six little indentations." I glance up at my friends' anxious faces.

"The alphabet!" Rosie gasps.

"That's it!" says Evelyn, sounding energized. "Each hole corresponds to a letter of the alphabet. Like a keyboard."

Alonso nods. "All we need to do is figure out the code, punch it into the honeycomb, and the box will open."

"But the code could be *anything*," I say, running my index finger along the ruffled ridge of the honeycomb. "Any series of letters, or even a word. But which one?"

We all rack our brains for a moment.

"Try 'Hornet,'" Drew suggests.

It's worth a shot. But first we have to decide whether the honeycomb alphabet would be set up like a standard "qwerty" keyboard or just plain alphabetically.

"My money's on the alphabet," says Louisa.

I'm inclined to agree with her, or at least, I hope she's right, because frankly, having to picture the letter positions on a keyboard and then hunt-and-peck my way through an invisible one would be a real pain. "Let's go with that," I decide.

Fingers tingling with excitement, I drag my fingernail across the pattern, ticking off the letters in a whisper. *H* is the eighth letter, and therefore the eighth "cup." I press my fingertip into the cup, and sure enough, I feel the bottom of it release and snap back into place, making the slightest clicking sound. Blood pounding in my ears, I count to the fifteenth little indentation, which would correspond to the letter *O*; again there is the click as the bottom of the cup presses in and pushes back.

"Is it working?" Rosie asks.

"We're definitely on the right track," I tell her. "I just hope 'Hornet' is the password."

I keep going; once I've made my way through the next four letters, we all hold our breath as I give the box a twist.

Nothing. The disappointment nearly knocks the wind out of me.

Ryan shrugs. "Maybe it was too obvious."

"Or maybe it's case sensitive?" Alonso suggests.

"Good thought," I say, "but there are only twenty-six honeycomb cups, so there's no shift key."

"It's got to be a different word, then," Evelyn says. "Think, Maddie. Your mom's password has to be one she'd never forget, a word that would mean something to her."

I frown. Ryan made a good point about "Hornet" being too obvious. A code word has to have some element of secrecy to it. When I changed my locker combination to a password, I wanted to just go with "Maddie," but Mom said that if anyone ever wanted to break in, that would be the first thing they'd try. So we came up with a word that only I would know, a word I could never forget.

I let out a little yelp of excitement. "I've got it!"

"What is it?" Jonah asks.

But I don't answer. I'm already counting off the cups, making my way through the alphabet to the letter *S*.

Then to *P.*

Then *A.*

My fingers are moving swiftly and gracefully, because I'm certain I am right.

R click.

R click.

It's the word I used for my locker combination. The word that was not just a word but a nickname. My nickname.

I press the *O*, and then, with a rush of confidence, the *W.*

Sparrow.

And then I feel it — deep within the little box, a series of mechanical *clack*s, a tumbling of gears.

I give the honeycomb a sharp twist and it releases, falling open into two perfect hollow halves lined with shiny copper.

Everyone leans in to see so fast that Drew and Alonso clonk heads.

The object that falls out is slender and silver, as light as a feather.

"It's a flash drive!" cries Louisa.

We hear the *thud-draaaaggg-thump-clunk* of Dizzy returning. He has waters for each of us, but he freezes when he sees the open honeycomb box — and flash drive — in my hand.

"Is that meant for your mother?" he asks me softly. He points to the box, adding, "I recognize that pattern. Symbols of the Hornet are used throughout the Resistance. It's likely it was your mother who even encoded that box and it's been passed along to different soldiers."

I nod, telling Dizzy, as I'd told Drew and Alonso, about Ivan asking me to pass the contents of the box on to my mother.

"I really want to see what's *on* the flash drive, so I can figure out where she is," I explain determinedly.

Dizzy studies me like he did before. "You really do look like her," he says.

"Thanks," I say, ducking my head.

"You're welcome. I see a little of your dad in you, too, though."

I feel a jolt of shock and happiness. Louisa gasps, too. "You know my father?" I ask.

"I do. Half the intelligence we have on the Alliance is a direct result of your dad's communication interception work," says Dizzy, his eyes resting on the flash drive. "So you can bet that whatever's on that is highly classified and heavily encoded."

I nod, my thoughts racing. So there's a good chance my parents are together.

"But wouldn't Ivan have encoded the drive?" Rosie points out, tossing her dark hair over one shoulder.

"Probably," Dizzy says. "But it would definitely be something only the Hornet or those closest to her would know how to crack."

"But to read it in the first place," Alonso muses out loud, "we're going to need a computer. And we don't even have access to one right now."

Dizzy's eyes shine with purpose. "As a matter of fact," he says, "we do."

Chapter 5

The *press box*, it's called, this room high above the field, looking out from behind home plate. The entire front of it consists of various-sized glass windows, most of which, miraculously, are still in one piece. There is a long counter with chairs pushed up to it. And on the counter there are six laptop computers.

Old ones.

Like *antiques*.

"Look at these dinosaurs," says Drew in amazement. "I bet they don't even have a 3-D function."

"What's the memory like?" Alonso asks, sitting down in front of one of the computers. "I bet it's some pathetically tiny amount, like, maybe twenty-three or twenty-four gigabytes."

Louisa laughs. "Oh, please. My preschool laptop had, like, twice that."

Dizzy snorts as he carefully takes a seat at one of the computers. "These babies, which were state of the art when they got left behind here, are probably about eight GB at the most."

"Wow," says Drew. "That's actually kind of sad."

"Will they be able to read the flash drive?" I ask, concerned.

"All we can do is try," says Dizzy, hitting a button and waiting as the computer whirs to life.

I sit down beside Dizzy and wring my hands. Everyone gathers around us, holding their breaths. Dizzy inserts the flash drive, and types in some commands.

The screen goes dark.

I swallow hard, and feel Louisa squeeze my shoulder.

And then, in the next second, the screen brightens, slowly, steadily, to a brilliant yellow. A black speck in the center expands into a swirl, which morphs into three broad black lines.

"The Hornet's symbol!" Ryan says.

Under the symbol, in bold caps, are the words: SECURITY CLEARANCE — LEVEL 10. CLASSIFICATION: MAX.

Then there is a place for another password.

Of course. I glance at Dizzy for assistance. But he's wincing and reaching down to massage his leg.

"Are you okay?" I ask him.

"I've done a lot of walking today," he says, and it's clear he's in a lot of pain. "More than usual."

"Why don't you go rest?" Louisa, ever the doctors' kid, suggests gently.

"Yeah," says Drew, "we'll come get you if we get stuck."

Dizzy clearly feels bad for bailing on us but his eyes show that he's in near agony. He gives us a superquick tutorial to familiarize us with the laptop, then wishes us luck and limps off. To me, it's a reminder of what our soldiers — the regular army and the Resistance alike —

are sacrificing for the safety of our country. I find myself wanting to help more than ever.

Unfortunately, I've never been much of a computer nerd. I confess this to my friends.

"Evelyn can do it," Alonso suggests. "She's got a way with these things."

Evelyn smiles and her cheeks turn slightly pink as she slides into the chair vacated by Dizzy. Louisa and the boys pull up some chairs. Rosie hops up onto the counter, with her legs dangling.

"Okay, it wants a password," she says, flexing her fingers.

"'Sparrow' again?" Louisa guesses. I'd filled in her and the others about that as we'd gone up to the press box.

"Probably not," says Rosie, turning to me. "Remember what Dizzy said? That Ivan would have encoded it, but it would be something your mom would probably know."

Words tumble through my mind. What would be something Ivan and Mom would both know?

"How about 'Resistance'?" I offer hopefully.

Evelyn types the word in quickly. Instantly, a message comes up: PASSWORD DENIED. AFTER TWO MORE INCORRECT PASSWORD ATTEMPTS, DATA WILL BE PERMANENTLY DELETED.

My stomach sinks. This is bad. I exchange glances with the others. We can't guess wildly now. We have to be very, very careful.

I close my eyes and drift back to the last day I saw my mother, the day she was deployed. I was sulking and feeling selfish and angry. I asked her why she had to go. And she answered me with a single word.

My eyes fly open. "Try 'freedom,'" I say.

Dutifully, Evelyn types in the word.

The cursor blinks once . . . twice. . . .

This is it. If *freedom* doesn't work, then we only have one more shot before we lose everything.

The cursor blinks once more. . . .

Then the black lines disappear in a burst of white.

We're in!

We all cheer. Louisa grabs me in a hug and Ryan and Jonah high-five again.

A document comes up on the screen.

Unfortunately, it's written entirely in code.

"Seriously?" Evelyn groans.

Drew leans closer, squinting at the screen. "It's like someone took a bunch of ancient hieroglyphics, translated them into a foreign language, then wrote them backward . . . with typos."

It's a pretty accurate description. Numbers and mathematical symbols alongside pictograms . . . inverted, transposed, repeated, upside down . . . It's exhausting to look at. Everyone breathes a collective sigh of frustration.

"No way we're going to figure this out," mutters Evelyn, flopping back in the chair and folding her arms across her chest. "Not without a cipher or a legend."

"You mean like the legend of the mutants?" asks Ryan, confused.

"No," says Rosie, rolling her eyes and poking him in the Cubs patch on the front of his borrowed uniform. "A legend is like a key, a cheat sheet for breaking codes."

"I knew that," Ryan grumbles.

"There has to be a legend," I say, reasoning it out, "and since this flash drive was going to my mother, she must be the one who has it."

Drew taps his foot, thinking. "I'll bet anything there's a second one. You know, a redundancy safeguard."

"Oooh, big words," jokes Rosie, causing him to blush.

"But he's right!" says Evelyn. "The Resistance would never allow just one copy of the legend to exist. I mean, sure, this is intended to be delivered into the hands of the Hornet. But if something ever went wrong, like, if something happened to her —"

She is cut off by a jab from Rosie's elbow.

"Evelyn!" gasps Louisa. "Shhh!"

The boys are all looking awkwardly elsewhere.

Evelyn instantly recognizes what she's said, and when she whirls to face me, she looks ready to burst into tears. "Oh, Maddie. I'm so sorry! I didn't mean —"

I hold up my hands and smile bravely. "It's okay. I know what you meant." I swallow my fear and nod to her. "Keep going."

71

She takes a moment to compose herself. "What I was going to say was that in addition to the cipher she carries with her, the Hornet would have to keep a second copy of the legend *somewhere*, for" — she chooses her next words carefully — "emergency purposes. Maybe the information is stored on a similar flash drive. There's probably some cool overlay compatibility function that will combine the two documents and translate —" She breaks off, sighing. "Well, I suppose it doesn't matter, since I don't know how we can get it."

The press box goes quiet, and when the silence is broken, it's my voice that does it.

"Maybe I do."

"Absolutely not!" says Louisa.

"I agree with Louisa," says Rosie.

"And I agree with Rosie," says Evelyn.

Louisa is standing in front of me and she's clamping her hands on my shoulders. "No way are you going to your apartment, Madeleine Frye."

"Yes," I say, for the eight billionth time in the last half hour. "I am."

I slide a sideways glance at Jonah. He hasn't said a word, but he's been pacing around the press box, looking concerned.

"C'mon, Maddie," says Ryan. "We've been saying all along that going home is a bad idea. The Alliance will have people waiting for us."

"It's too great a risk," Drew chimes in.

"Would you rather the Resistance doesn't get this flash drive?" I ask them in my most reasonable tone. "Would you rather we don't find my mom and Wren?"

Of course, no one wants that at all.

"Then it's settled." I stand up, surprised by the authority in my voice. "If my mother has a second legend, our apartment is where it will be. So I'm going home to see if I can find it. It's the one hope we have of reaching my mom to give her this information."

"Fine," says Louisa, flinging her arms wide in a gesture of surrender. "But if you're going, I'm going."

"And if she's going," says Ryan, in a protective tone, "I'm going."

Louisa gives him a sweet smile and Ryan turns bright red, all the way up to his ears.

Jonah stops pacing and comes to squat down beside my chair, putting us eye to eye.

"If you're going, I'm going," he says softly, and now I'm smiling, too.

But the mood is broken in the next second when everyone starts talking at once, volunteering and offering reasons why *they* should be allowed to go, until finally, Drew puts his fingers in his mouth and lets out one of those ear-piercing, attention-getting whistles that shuts everyone up.

"We can't all go," says Drew.

"He's right," I say. "So would anyone like to hear what I think?"

They all nod.

"Okay . . ." I pause to collect my thoughts. I'm usually not this logical, but the situation isn't leaving me much choice. "It's actually a plus that we know there will be

Alliance agents lying in wait, because we can plan around that. I think I need to bring two people — no more, no less. One to go inside with me and another to stand lookout."

"I'll be the lookout," says Jonah, in a decisive tone. "Nonnegotiable. Me."

I nod, and keep going. "And I think Louisa should be the one to go inside the apartment with me. I mean, she knows my place as well as I do, so that's bound to be helpful, right?"

"Good point," says Evelyn.

"Okay," says Rosie. "It's settled. Louisa and Jonah will go with Maddie tomorrow and see if they can find anything that will help us crack this code." She turns a smile to me. "Good thinking, Maddie. I couldn't have come up with a better plan myself."

Her words are the best affirmation I could have hoped for. Evelyn is also looking impressed.

"What will we do?" asks Alonso.

"You mean besides pray?" sighs Louisa.

"I think you guys should work on a strategy," I say,

"for what we'll do on the outside chance that the information we need isn't waiting somewhere in my apartment."

We make a plan for Jonah, Louisa, and me to leave the stadium just before sunrise, to avoid as much of the commuting crowd as we can.

By now, everyone is exhausted, so we retire to the home team's and visitors' lockers. We use our sleeping bags, which Drew and Alonso toted from the car wash, and extra uniforms and Cubs windbreakers for additional blankets and pillows.

In a matter of moments, Rosie, Evelyn, and Louisa are sound asleep. But as tired as I am, I lie awake, thinking. Back at home, on nights when I couldn't fall asleep, I'd take out my puzzle book and try to solve one of the harder ones my mom had devised for me. Sometimes I'd even attempt to make up my own cryptogram, but I'd usually fall asleep halfway through.

But now thinking about puzzles only tightens the knots in my stomach. Just getting from Wrigley to my apartment tomorrow is going to be dangerous enough, but I'll be walking willingly into the direct sights of hostile Alliance spies.

But I've got to do it.

Because somewhere back in my apartment there just might be the key to finding my mother.

Chapter 6

Louisa, Jonah, and I set out early. The sky is streaked dull gray and pale yellow, and a ghostly wind howls around the walls of Wrigley Field.

We've left the others sleeping. Dizzy limps to the exit with us, and gives us some last-minute reminders. He also gives me a special tool in case I need to pick the lock on our apartment door, which is good since I don't have a key. As we walk away from the stadium I don't look back, but I can feel his concerned gaze on us; I'm sure he's still standing there long after we turn the corner and vanish from his sight.

We head northwest toward my apartment building. In the crumbling town houses that line the streets, only a

78

few windows are lit. I imagine sleepy employees getting ready for the early work shift or a world-weary insomniac sitting quietly in the early-morning gloom, wondering what will become of all of us.

Jonah is no stranger to the streets at this hour, so I give him the address and we let him take the lead. I can tell Louisa is terrified, jumping at every sound. She hugs herself against the brutal slicing of the wind and stays close at my heels. It occurs to me how courageous of her it was to volunteer for this mission. And how incredibly loyal. How could I have ever doubted her?

We pass an alley, and I get the distinct feeling there are eyes staring out at us. I walk a little faster. The buildings cast deep, charcoal-toned shadows, which make everything much creepier.

"It's too dark," Louisa says, clearly sharing my thoughts. "Why don't we walk up on the L tracks? We'll have better visibility."

"And fewer dark alleys," Jonah adds.

I nod at them, feeling grateful that they've thought of this.

The elevated trains haven't run in years, not since the government decided it required too much energy to run them. The three of us carefully take the stairs to the elevated tracks. As we walk along the rusted rails, rats scuttle along at the far edges of the platform, and occasionally a filthy pigeon will swoop down so close I can actually see its beady little oil-slick eyes.

"At least we don't have to worry about a train coming at us," Louisa remarks.

The words are barely out of her mouth when I notice something approaching from the opposite direction, following the tracks at a steady, purposeful pace.

Heading right for us.

I squint into the growing daylight, hoping my eyes are playing tricks on me. But they aren't.

There is something moving toward us, all right. On a collision course.

It is definitely not a train.

But I almost wish it were.

Jonah immediately puts himself in front of Louisa

and me. He pushes his shoulders back and I can see his hands flex into fists at his sides. His whole body is tensed, his jaw set in a menacing expression.

"Daggers," he says through his teeth.

My knees wobble. Louisa actually lets out a whimper.

They are getting closer and I can see that these swaggering strangers — a quick count gives me three boys and two girls — are not an especially friendly bunch.

It's strange to see kids of their age, which I guess to be between seventeen and eighteen, out in the world, because it's mandatory for anyone over the age of fifteen to enlist in the military. Not doing so is punishable by imprisonment. Clearly, the Daggers have found a way to dodge not only the draft but the police as well.

Out in front is, I assume, the leader. He has a tall, stiff bristle of jet-black hair running right down the middle of his head from front to back. Around his eyes are two black smudges that look as though he's darkened them with soot. He has a tattoo encircling his throat that I think is supposed to look like barbed wire.

Lovely.

Behind him is a shorter boy, whom I take to be the second in command. His squat body is a knot of sheer muscle. He has stringy hair bleached perfectly white.

The two girls come next. The one on the right is pretty, with a metal hoop pierced into her lower lip and another in her eyebrow. She wears tattered jeans and a pair of yellow leather boots that come midway up her thighs. The girl to her left is dressed head to toe in shiny red vinyl — cap, jacket, and boots. She has slick black gloss on her lips and heavy green shadow smeared on her eyelids.

The last boy in the group has long dreadlocks and he wears a frayed denim jacket painted with a jewel-handled blade under which, in fierce silver calligraphy, is the word *Daggers*.

I guess that's to remind him, in case he forgets who his friends are?

They stop, about four feet in front of us. The short, muscular one says, "This is Dagger territory."

Dreadlocks tugs a chain from where it's looped over his shoulder and begins to swing it in slow circles.

I might throw up. I might faint. I might jump from the elevated tracks and take my chances with gravity.

"Look at the little angels," says the leader in a scornful tone. "Where you going? Sunday school?"

"Let us by," says Jonah, his voice a low growl.

I'm shocked when the girl in the yellow boots darts behind me, flings out one long leg, and connects gracefully with the backs of my knees. It doesn't hurt, but it does cause me to crumble to the ground. Louisa shrieks and Jonah lunges for the nearest gang member — the leader. Unfortunately, the über-muscular one darts out to place himself between Jonah and his target. He's got the element of surprise on his side, and for Jonah, it's like hitting a brick wall. Jonah goes down hard.

"Please don't hurt us," says Louisa in a strangled voice.

"You got any valuables, little princess?" the girl in red vinyl demands of her, then slices a glare my way.

I've managed to get back on my feet. "No, we don't!" My heart is pounding so hard I'm afraid it might explode. I adjust the Cubs cap on my head.

Now Jonah has hauled himself up from the tracks and comes to stand beside me, shaking off his spill and looking like he's not going to get caught by surprise like that a second time. His eyes are like steel.

"We're just passing through this neighborhood," he says. There is authority in his voice, like when he spoke to Brianna.

"If you're planning to rob us, that would be a waste of your time," he goes on. "We have nothing for you to take."

The leader's eyes are burning with fury, but so far he's not doing anything. Maybe it's Jonah's height and broad shoulders that are making him think twice.

The girl in the red vinyl — obviously the most fashion forward of the gang — is looking at my Cubs uniform intently, admiring it. I see an opportunity.

"Do you like this?" I ask quickly, indicating the jersey. "I've got, like, a hundred more like it back where I came from." I hope I don't sound as terrified as I feel.

Luckily, Louisa and I both put on our long-sleeved shirts under our jerseys before we left this morning. As if it's the most natural thing in the world, I tug the jersey over my head and hand it to Red Vinyl Girl. "Take it," I say.

She looks at the leader, for permission, I guess. He gives a curt nod and she takes the shirt. I don't get a thank-you. Not that I was expecting one.

Now Yellow Boots looks jealous. I motion to Louisa to hand over her jersey, which she does. Fast.

Then the leader slowly raises his fingers to his lips, like Drew did last night. His soot-smudged eyes bore into me a long moment before he whistles. It's a quick blast, high and loud. He follows it with two more short ones, then a long one.

Nothing happens at first.

Then I hear it. A distant thumping sound, coming from the same direction the Daggers had. It's a galloping noise, and as it draws closer, there is another sound.

Barking.

"Oh no," says Louisa.

I know she's remembering the dogs we saw in the road yesterday on our way to Wrigley Field. And I'm trembling now because I'm pretty sure no amount of Jonah's slick talking is going to work on a pack of wild animals.

They barrel into view, a gray and brown haze of fur, teeth, and claws. They charge toward us, growling and snapping.

Without even thinking, I push Louisa and Jonah behind me, just as the first dog reaches us. Ears back, teeth bared, he leaps, taking me down onto the tracks with a thud.

I cover my head with my arms and open my mouth to scream.

But there are no teeth sinking into my flesh, no claws tearing at my face and hair. Just a big tongue lapping at my cheeks, and a cold nose nuzzling my ears. I remove my hands from my head and look at the dog. His big brown eyes are filled with nothing but love.

Two more of his canine cohorts join him now, pushing themselves onto my lap and rubbing their furry ears against my face. I'm still trembling, my body not catching up to my mind. *We're not in danger.*

"Our pets," the leader explains. "They're trained to attack only on command."

He steps forward and reaches down to give the first dog a gentle nudge, removing him from my lap so I can stand up.

Yellow Boots claps her hands twice. Without hesitation, the dogs sit. Hesitantly, Louisa crouches down to pet a small, black-spotted dog. He stretches his neck for her to scratch.

"Amazing," says Jonah.

I see that the girl in the red vinyl has slipped the jersey on over her shiny jacket. She gives me a shy look. Not quite a thank-you, but close.

Now there is a silence in which something passes between Jonah and the leader — a look, an understanding, a mutual stand-down.

Jonah nods at Louisa and me. "Let's go," he says.

As we leave, a couple of them nod at us; the girl in red even waves. The leader actually smiles.

It's a nice smile.

For some reason, it makes me hate the War more than ever.

It's a long walk, but at least we don't cross paths with any other people. The streets below are beginning to look familiar, and I recognize the buildings rising up from them in varying degrees of decay. We've reached my neighborhood.

We clamber down the El stairs. The moment my feet hit the pavement I feel such a wave of emotion I have to stop walking. The feeling is a mixture of sadness and joy, terror and comfort. I learned to ride my bike on this street; I watched my mother board the bus that took her to war at this corner.

"Are you sure you want to do this, Maddie?" Louisa asks.

"I have to do this," I say, as much to myself as to her. A few more yards and my building will come into view. The pull is magnetic.

Louisa and I are wearing Cubs caps, which shade our faces pretty well. We've both smushed our hair up under the caps, and we're wearing partial, baggy baseball uniforms. I hope all these efforts will make us look like boys. They aren't the greatest disguises in the world (especially without the jerseys), but they were the best we could do. If the Alliance spies are looking for a girl to return to this address, maybe this will at least throw them off a little.

We pass the place on the sidewalk where I fell down Rollerblading; six stitches in my left elbow.

There's the old mailbox Joey Dennison hid behind every time we neighborhood kids played hide-and-seek.

And there's the stoop where old Mrs. Lorenzo sat and cried when she heard that her grandson was lost in the first wave of the War.

Home.

I spot the first Alliance operative almost immediately.

"Spy," I say quietly, inclining my head to make the most of the cap's brim. "There, by the mailbox."

Jonah and Louisa look. There's a woman in an official government mail carrier's uniform, lingering beside Joey's favorite hiding place, pretending to shuffle through the parcels in her bag.

"Are you sure?" asks Jonah. "She looks pretty legit to me."

But she's not. "Snail mail" (as Mom said they used to call it) is pretty much obsolete, but there are still some things — like the packages in the phony mail carrier's bag — that just can't be sent electronically. So a few years ago, the government designated the postal system for that purpose. A handful of these federal mailboxes are still in use around the city to accommodate small packages, but they're few and far between. And what Jonah and the Alliance operative don't know is that this particular mailbox hasn't been operational since Joey's twin brother, Ricky, stuffed an entire brick of firecrackers into it on the last Fourth of July before both he and Joey went off to join the army.

I continue to scan the area. There is a construction worker examining a pothole in the street, directly in front of the main entrance to my building.

"He's a fake, too," I whisper.

"How do you know?" Louisa whispers back.

"Almost no one in this part of town drives anymore, so why would the city waste valuable resources fixing the road?"

"Is there a rear entrance to your building?" Jonah wonders.

"Yes," I say. "But I'm sure the Alliance is watching that one, too. I mean, you don't take control of Canada by being lazy." I figure the Alliance must be sending different spies, in different guises, here every day. Otherwise, neighbors would start to get suspicious.

"How are we going to get in, then?" Louisa hisses.

I spot the alleyway that runs between my building and the one next door, where the Dennisons live. Joey's bedroom window is directly across the alley from mine. Sometimes we would open our windows and chat. Joey is two years older than me, but he was always sweet, and Louisa was convinced he had a crush on me. I doubt it, but Louisa always says she's right about these things.

"Remember Joey and Ricky?" Louisa whispers. She sometimes seems capable of reading my mind — I guess that's what happens after being friends for so many years.

I nod tersely, wanting to tell Louisa this isn't the time or place for a trip down memory lane.

But Louisa goes on. "Didn't you say you and Joey used to see Ricky sneaking home late at night, using the fire escape?"

I turn to Louisa, nodding more slowly this time.

Her blue eyes are bright. "I have an idea."

The Alliance mail carrier is still lingering by the mailbox and the Alliance construction worker is trying to look busy, staring at the stupid pothole.

"There are only two of them," says Jonah, who's already made it clear that he is not on board with my plan, even a little. "There are three of us. Maybe we can . . ."

I shake my head. "I'm willing to bet that under that postal uniform and construction vest, they are heavily armed."

I'm not used to being the one making decisions. It's a little bit nerve-racking. It's also kind of exciting.

We are walking down the sidewalk toward Joey's building, looking — we hope — like three ordinary boys.

"What floor did you say you live on again?" Jonah asks.

"Ninth," I say with forced cheerfulness.

"Great."

The spies may be watching my building, but nobody is watching Joey's. The construction guy is still pretending to be deeply involved with the hole in the asphalt when Mrs. Lorenzo's chatty daughter, Jackie, exits her building. She's probably on her way to pick up more

Butter Brickle non-dairy ice cream product for her mother. Jackie approaches the mail carrier and begins a conversation.

This is a very lucky break. I know from experience that Jackie Lorenzo can talk for hours. She's pointing to the mailbox and asking questions. It's just the distraction we need.

Jonah, the lookout, will use his Phoenix School whistle to alert us if there is any change in status. Taking advantage of Jackie's presence, Louisa and I make our way across the street. It takes every inch of willpower we have not to break into a run, but since that would call attention to us, we force ourselves to walk.

We make it to the entrance of Joey's apartment building without the postal carrier or the construction worker noticing.

"Does someone have to buzz us in?" Louisa asks under her breath, when we arrive at the glass doors of the main entrance.

"Used to," I say, pulling open the heavy door. "They

did away with the buzzers years ago to save power." Another lucky break.

On the other, *unlucky* hand, they also did away with the elevators for the same reason. So we have to walk the nine flights up to Joey's floor.

I'm hoping we don't run into any of the apartment building's inhabitants who might recognize me. Louisa's original plan had been to avoid the halls, the stairwell, and the lobby by climbing up the fire escape. But unlike Ricky, we aren't tall enough to jump up and tug the fire escape ladder down. We have every intention of using the fire escape as our way out, though.

Calf muscles throbbing, we push through the stairwell door and into the ninth-floor corridor.

Here's where it gets dicey: Joey and Ricky are away at military training camp in California. Mr. Dennison is off serving his mandatory military tour overseas, and isn't due back until early next spring. The only wild card is Mrs. Dennison. She was exempted from military duty because she had lost hearing in one ear as a child, so she works part-time at the local grocery store, but I don't remember her schedule. I do remember she was a neat freak: always obsessed with cleaning the apartment, ironing, and keeping their laundry looking sharp even with the city's strict water-rationing policy and electrical shortages. I figure we've got a fifty-fifty shot at her being out at this time of day.

If she's home, this whole mission will be an epic fail.

"You knock on the door," I tell Louisa. "Mrs. Dennison's never met you, so you can just pretend you're lost or something."

Louisa makes her way to apartment 9D and knocks gently on the door.

We wait.

"Knock a little louder," I whisper from where I'm hiding behind a huge potted plastic plant.

Louisa knocks again. After a good two minutes with no response from inside, we feel pretty confident that Mrs. Dennison is not at home. I join Louisa at the door and make quick work of the bolt with Dizzy's handy-dandy lock picker.

And then we're inside.

I pause in the tiny entranceway and breathe in the scent I remember as distinctly as my own name: the lingering aroma of that morning's tofu bacon mixed with the clean, crisp scent of the rosewater spray starch Mrs. Dennison uses when she irons.

We go directly to Joey's old room. Louisa flings open the window that leads to the fire escape, while I search for something heavy enough to smash my bedroom window, but not too heavy for me to hurl across the alley.

I look around the room frantically. There's Joey's prized possession — his laptop — but I can't bring myself to fling that out the window. There are a handful of sports trophies, but none big enough to break the glass (Joey never was much of an athlete). There is a small lamp with a plastic base (useless). Then Louisa spots it — wedged in the corner: a bowling ball.

I go out on the fire escape with it. Hoisting the heavy orb up to my shoulder, I send it shot-put style across the alley and through the plate glass of my bedroom window.

I can only hope no one comes running at the sound of the glass shattering. But I guess since we're nine stories up, no one hears it. And speaking of nine stories up . . .

I try not to look down as I gauge the distance from Joey's window to my own. The alley is only about six feet wide, and the fire escape landing closes that gap by about two and a half feet. So according to my calculations, I'll have to clear only about three and a half feet when I jump from the fire escape landing and through my bedroom window.

That's right: *jump*.

Louisa sees me eyeing the distance and she begins to get jittery. "Um, Maddie, I think I'm having second thoughts about this part of the plan."

So am I. It's not just the height and the distance that scare me; it's the shards of broken glass still stuck in the window frame that are really giving me pause. Even if I make it across the alley, and through the window, those glass fragments are going to be hard to miss.

And that's *if* I even make it across.

Again, I look around Joey's room, this time for something I can use to fashion a makeshift bridge. It has to be at least four feet long and strong enough to hold me and Louisa. Separately, of course. But Joey's room is turning out to be a major disappointment.

Frustrated, I throw myself onto Joey's bed, facedown into his pillowcase.

His crisp, rose-scented, meticulously *ironed* pillowcase.

I spring up and tell Louisa to wait here while I dash out of the room.

Minutes later, I'm back, lugging our bridge.

Chapter 7

Are you crazy?" Louisa demands. "You want to walk across the alley on an ironing board?"

"An *industrial-grade* ironing board," I correct her, struggling to maneuver the giant laundry apparatus out the window and onto the fire escape. "Mrs. Dennison was always very clear about that."

With great effort, I balance the wide end of the board on the railing of the fire escape and lower the narrow end out across the alley until it lands on my windowsill. I give it a little jiggle to test it.

"Sturdy," I pronounce.

Louisa does not look convinced.

So I climb up onto the board and carefully take a

step away from the fire escape landing. "See? Perfectly safe."

I begin making my way across the padded surface of the board, putting one foot painstakingly in front of the other and holding out my arms for balance. *Don't look down don't look down don't look down*, I tell myself, my blood roaring in my ears. I remember at CMS Evelyn told me she was scared of heights. I never have been, but I think that could all change right now.

At last, I reach the windowsill. Taking care to avoid the broken glass pieces, I duck in the window and hop down, landing safely on my bedroom floor.

My bedroom floor.

I look around the room, tears blurring my vision for a moment. It's all so painfully familiar, but alien at the same time. The light yellow walls, the scuffed pink dresser, the ancient stuffed animals, my bed . . .

My bed.

I fight the urge to drop onto my mattress and dive under the fluffy, oversized comforter I've always loved. I know if I do that, I will be crushed under the weight of more emotion than I'm ready to bear. If I do that, I will never be able to make myself leave.

Focus, I tell myself. *This is a mission. See it through.*

"That was amazing," cries Louisa, gawking at me across the alleyway. "You're so brave. You weren't scared at all."

"Louisa, I was terrified." I yank open a dresser drawer, feeling a sting of memory at the sight of a few old T-shirts in there — the ones I didn't like enough to bring with me to Louisa's. I grab a ratty one, wrap it around my hand, and carefully punch the pointy glass shards out of the window frame, sweeping away the tiny broken pieces from the sill. "Brave doesn't mean not being scared," I tell Louisa, who's about to step out onto the ironing board. "Bravery is just, I don't know, doing what you have to do, even when you're scared to death." As the words come out of my mouth, I realize they almost sound like something . . . my mother would say.

Louisa takes a deep breath. "Okay," she says. "Then here's me, doing what I have to do."

I clamp my hands around the edges of the ironing

board and hold tight, giving the bridge some extra support. Louisa, the athlete, is graceful and coordinated and she makes it across without incident.

"Now what?" she says, letting out a breath as she joins me inside. She looks around my room and her blue eyes fill with the same kind of nostalgia that's making my heart ache.

"We search," I say, bottling back the tears building in me. "Evelyn seemed to think the legend would be on a flash drive, so we can start by looking for one of those."

We exit my room and head to the living room. Everything looks the same. On the row of hooks by the front door hang my father's favorite sweatshirt and our three mandatory gas masks. Posted on the back of the door is the building's emergency escape route, and below that an evacuation map of Chicago, to be used during citywide invasion drills. There's a pair of old sneakers in the middle of the floor, right where I'd left them the day I moved in with the Ballingers. Above the mantel is the stark, black-on-white abstract painting that's hung there for as long as I can remember.

Both my parents like modern art, but since we could never afford the genuine article, we made do with inexpensive prints and reproductions. Before the Art Institute was burned, Mom and Dad would take me there on day trips, eager for me to learn about all kinds of art. We even saw a concert once, in the Institute's Rubloff Auditorium. My mother liked to say that the Institute was just "buzzing" with artistic energy, like a hive of creative geniuses.

"I always loved coming to your house," Louisa suddenly says, her voice wistful.

"Really?" This comes as a shock to me. Louisa's house is big and beautiful, with decorator furniture and a sprawling yard out back.

"Don't get me wrong," says Louisa, following me to the kitchen. "I mean, I love my family and my home, but your apartment was always so cozy. I loved that when we were falling asleep in your room, we could hear your parents laughing together in the living room. And there were always kids playing out in the street. You could never be lonely here."

For the first time it occurs to me that maybe Louisa didn't have everything in the world, like I'd always thought.

"We should get started," Louisa says, snapping out of her thoughts.

I nod. "Try my mom's desk."

Louisa goes to the corner of the living room that my parents use as a home office area. She sets about searching through the desk drawers while I head for my parents' bedroom.

It's pretty bare — they took most of their belongings. I check my mother's jewelry box. She's never had any really fancy or expensive jewelry like Dr. Ballinger, who has an antique strand of pearls and lots of gold rings and bracelets. I search all the felt-lined compartments — no flash drive.

I fling open the closet doors and riffle through her pants pockets, jacket linings, and purses; I shake all of her shoes hoping a flash drive will fall out of one of them. No such luck.

I go back into the living room. Louisa is looking

105

under the sofa cushions. She turns to me and says, "Nothing." I can see she's starting to panic. So am I.

"Maybe it's not a flash drive," I say, grasping at straws.

"Well, what else could it be?"

Good question. I let my eyes scan the living room, wondering if there might be anything in here that could provide a means of decoding the document. My eyes are drawn to the huge abstract painting above the mantel.

And I have to catch my breath.

Because only now do I realize what that painting really is: *lines!* Bold black stripes arranged in groups of three, parallel and equidistant, a repeating pattern.

They are the symbol of the Hornet!

So it was always there, always in my life. This legacy, this promise. My mother's courage and dedication represented in three black lines, like a secret family crest.

A crazy notion drives me to climb up on the mantel and reach for the painting. Maybe there's some numeric clue in the pattern of the lines, or perhaps it's as simple as the legend being printed on the back of the canvas. Or maybe there's a safe hidden behind the artwork and there's a flash drive inside it.

"Louisa!" I cry. "Give me a hand with this!"

It takes me a moment of struggling with the heavy canvas to realize that Louisa isn't helping me. I turn to look over my shoulder, ready to ask her why, and that's when I see that she's frozen in place, staring at the front door to the apartment.

Someone on the other side of it is turning the knob.

A tsunami of terror crashes over me. I hop down from the mantel and grab Louisa's arm, tugging her through the living room and back into my bedroom. I peek around the doorframe just as the front door opens.

I am expecting to see an Alliance scout or an armed police officer entering my apartment. So when I realize who it is, I nearly collapse with relief.

"Who's there?" Louisa whispers from where she's crouching behind my dresser.

My mouth and throat have suddenly gone dry, and I have to swallow before I answer. "It's your mother."

There in my living room stands Dr. Ballinger, the woman who's been like a second mom to me since kindergarten. She is an older version of Louisa, just as pretty, just as graceful. At first I can't imagine why on earth she would be in my apartment when both my parents are away and I, her phony daughter, am (as far as she knows) off at boarding school with her real one.

"What is she doing here?" I whisper to Louisa.

"Who cares?" Louisa's eyes are already shining with tears of happiness and relief. "All that matters is she's here. We don't have to run anymore!"

I wonder why this announcement doesn't have me jumping for joy.

Louisa reaches for the doorknob; instinctively I pull her back.

"What's *wrong* with you?" she hisses, scowling. "I want to see my mom!"

"So do I!" I whisper hurriedly. "But, I don't know. . . . Something is just telling me we shouldn't go out."

I don't know why but there's this powerful feeling of apprehension, like a silent alarm in my head telling me to remain hidden.

Louisa looks at me like I've lost my mind. "Maddie, all we've wanted all this time was to go home to our parents. And the only reason we couldn't do that was because we knew the Alliance would be watching and waiting to ambush us before we even made it in the door."

I nod. She's right, of course, but the warning lights are still flashing in my brain. "I just think we shouldn't," I whisper feebly. I couldn't explain why even if I tried. It's just a feeling, a hunch.

Louisa's whisper takes on an angry edge. "My mother will take care of us! She can call the authorities and explain about CMS; the military will search out the Alliance cells in the city and vaporize them!" She frowns. "We're saved, Maddie! I don't understand what you're waiting for!"

My lip trembles. "Don't you think I'd love to run out there now and throw myself into her arms, just as much as you would?"

Louisa's frown deepens and her voice is choked with tears. "So why don't we? And why are you being so bossy all of a sudden? Do you think just because your mom's a leader it gives you the right to be one, too?" she snaps. Suddenly her face changes. "That's it, isn't it? You don't want to go out there because it's *my* mother. You're *jealous* because my mother is *here*, while your mom is off being the Hornet. You can't see your mother so you don't want me to see mine!"

Her words are like a slap in the face. I feel the sting all the way to my heart. I try to speak but I can't. All I can do is shake my head.

Louisa turns away from me and is about to stomp out of the bedroom.

And that's when we hear the knock.

Chapter 8

Louisa stops dead in her tracks. I peer out again carefully, and I see Dr. Ballinger opening the apartment's front door.

On the other side is the construction worker–slash–Alliance spy.

My blood goes cold with fear. Dr. Ballinger is in danger! The operative must have recognized her when she entered the building — the Alliance surely has files and photos on all of us "escapees" and our families — and followed her inside.

"May I help you?" Louisa's mom asks courteously.

"Yes, ma'am," says the phony pothole specialist.

"We've had reports of a gas leak and I need to check all the apartments in the building."

I detect only a hint of an accent, one I can't place. I hold my breath, praying Dr. Ballinger won't let him in.

"I don't live here," she explains. "I'm only here to gather some things for the tenant's daughter, who's away at school with my daughter. You see, I heard on NewsServ that a severe cold front, somewhere in the eighty-below-zero range, is going to hit the entire Midwest region later this week, so I thought I should send some warmer clothing. . . ." She trails off, laughing self-consciously. Something about him must be making her nervous. I hope she realizes what's really going on, and can get out in time. "Oh, I'm sure you're not interested in that."

"No, ma'am," says the enemy.

Anguish fills me. My first thought is that even if Louisa and I manage to get out without the operative seeing us, we're still leaving Dr. B alone with him. But then I realize that the Alliance has known of the Ballingers' whereabouts — and the other parents, too — from the start. If they were going to cause them any harm, they'd have done so already. I'm sure the Alliance is convinced they'll be able to recapture us, a bunch of eighth-grade runaways, so it's still in their best interest to keep our parents alive and well. Then they'll be able to act on their original plan, which was to ransom us in exchange for the power and influence of our families.

Of course, if the spy finds us here *with* Dr. Ballinger, all bets are off. Who knows what he'd do to all three of us under those circumstances?

I explain this all to Louisa in a frantic whisper. She frowns, then nods just as we hear Dr. Ballinger telling the spy that he can come in. She suggests he begin his check in the kitchen, where the gas appliances are.

Thank goodness the kitchen and my bedroom are at completely opposite sides of the apartment.

"We have to go," I tell Louisa. "Now!"

She looks around desperately. "But we haven't found anything to help us decipher the code on the flash drive."

She's right, of course. I am so frustrated I could scream. Why does everything have to be so hard? It's like a giant puzzle, and *none* of the pieces are fitting together.

The word explodes in my mind: *puzzles!* Puzzles, codes, cryptograms, ciphers. I think of the crazy mess on Ivan's flash drive and the cryptograms in my puzzle book. Could it be that they're all connected?

The flash of hope nearly blinds me. I run to my night table, tug open the drawer, and grab the book my mother gave me so long ago.

Then I point to the window. Louisa is there in the blink of an eye. I help her onto the ironing board and she makes it across in seconds flat. She quickly unlatches the fire escape's sliding ladder, which we'll use to climb down to the alley. I am about to step onto the "bridge" when we hear a long, shrill whistle coming from the street.

Not the kind of whistle you execute by sticking your fingers in your mouth.

This is the kind that can only be produced by an official Phoenix School cadet whistle.

Jonah! The warning signal.

Sure enough, just as I duck back inside the bedroom window, I catch a glimpse of the mail carrier entering the alley from the street side. Louisa ducks into Joey's window just in the nick of time.

Like the construction worker, this spy must have seen Dr. Ballinger enter my building, and now she's checking the perimeter. I doubt she knows that Louisa and I are here, but she is definitely on alert.

And if she happens to glance upward, there's no way she'll miss the giant ironing board spanning the alley. I'm pretty sure that will pique her interest even further, and we can't have that.

I don't have time for thinking, only for action.

Quickly, I turn from the window and drag the heavy comforter from my bed, along with my sheets and pillow. Then I fling all that bedding out the window. My aim is good: the sheets and comforter land right on the mail carrier and cover her like a net, trapping her underneath. The element of surprise must also make her trip and land facedown.

In a heartbeat, Louisa appears on the fire escape landing again and swiftly lowers the ladder. Below us, the mail carrier is struggling to get out from under the bedding. I climb up onto the windowsill, grasping my puzzle book, but my hurry makes me clumsy and my fear makes my palms sweaty. The book slips from my hand at the same moment that I lose my footing, catching the ironing board with my heel, and nearly pitching forward out the window.

Louisa has clambered halfway down the ladder but stops to look across the alley at me with terror-filled eyes.

I manage to grab on to the window frame and regain my balance, but the ironing board is not so lucky. It wobbles, then drops, free-falling nine stories to land in the alley with a crash, right beside my puzzle book.

The noise of the crash scares the spy, who stops wriggling under the blanket for a moment.

My mind races as I consider my options, none of them good. I can hide here in my room and hope the Alliance spy (who is surely done with his pretend inspection of the kitchen and making his way to this side of the apartment) doesn't find me.

Or I can get out of this window somehow.

But how?

I could probably sail across the alley on an impromptu zip line, which I could fashion out of my old jump rope and a coat hanger.

Yeah, I could do that.

If I had, like, five hours to spare.

Clenching my teeth, I climb onto the windowsill.

I look across the alley.

I look down at the ground, nine floors below me, where the mail carrier is again trying to push the comforter off herself.

Bravery is doing what you have to do.

Even when you're scared to death.

Once again, there is no thought. Just action.

So I brace myself.

And jump.

I am airborne for mere seconds. But the sensation is a terrifying rush as I hurtle through a three-and-a-half-foot span of nothingness toward Joey Dennison's fire escape.

Unfortunately, I've misjudged the propulsion, and even in the fraction of a heartbeat it takes to soar across the alley, I know that I will fall short of my target. My feet are not going to make it to the landing.

All I can do is reach for the rail and hope I connect with it.

I stretch my arms out in front of me, leaning, reaching, fingers grasping. . . .

I hear Louisa gasp in horror one split second before I collide with the fire escape. But only one of my hands makes contact with the rail. Frantically, I close my fingers around the slender section of metal and hold on for dear life. I can already feel the burn in my biceps, the ache in my shoulder, as I dangle there by one arm, my own weight pulling me downward toward the cement of the alley beneath me.

"Don't let go!" Louisa cries.

I want to tell her to whisper — the Alliance agent can hear us — but right now I'm focused on surviving. My legs flail wildly as I attempt to swing them high enough to get a foothold on the landing. No luck. Somehow my baseball cap stays on my head. Sweat is pouring down my back. Then I hear Louisa clambering back up the metal rungs of the ladder.

"No!" I hiss at her. "There's no time. You have to get away."

But she's back on the landing now; she reaches over the rail to clasp her hand firmly around my wrist. "Give me your other hand!"

Somehow I manage to raise my other arm toward Louisa's outstretched hand. She catches it and holds tight, grunting as she hauls me upward.

My right knee reaches the edge of the landing, then my left, and I steady myself but I just can't find the power to lift myself any farther. My whole body is throbbing with pain.

"You have to get out of here," I command, my voice breaking on a sob. "Leave me!"

But my best friend does not let go. With her breath coming in strained gasps, Louisa summons a burst of superhuman strength and pulls me to my feet. I swing one leg, then the other, over the railing to safety. Panting with exhaustion and fear, I crumple to the metal grid floor of the fire escape.

Louisa helps me up and we hurry down the ladder. We're out of breath after nine stories. The second our feet hit the ground, the mail carrier manages to free herself from beneath the blanket. She stands up. When her eyes meet mine, the hatred in them is so immense that I go cold inside.

She touches her ear and speaks softly into what must be a communication device.

"Spotted: two boys in the alley. Possible fliers."

I feel a mix of relief and terror. She doesn't know who we really are. She thinks we're boys. But we're still about to be trapped, unless we flee now.

"Come on, come on," Louisa urges, tugging me toward the end of the alley.

"Wait!" I cry, pulling free of Louisa's hold. "The book!"

I take a tentative step in the direction of the book, which is lying less than a foot from the Alliance agent's toe. Her eyes are fixed on me as I approach. I don't think either of us is breathing.

Keeping my gaze locked with hers, I lean down slowly, slowly. . . .

My fingertips touch the spine of the book. In a lightning-fast movement, I snatch it up and spin away, ready to run. . . .

"Aaaaaghhh!"

A raging bellow erupts from her. In a whiplike motion, her hand lashes out and clamps around my elbow like a vise. I stumble, almost dropping my book. That's it. I'm caught.

Then I hear a boy's voice call out from behind us.

"Hey, you Alliance creep!" he shouts.

It's Jonah. His voice seems to echo off the bricks of the buildings.

The spy and I turn around to see him standing at the mouth of the alley. Then he takes off at top speed across the street and down a narrow side road.

The spy looks from me back to Jonah, clearly torn about what to do. Then, a split second later, she charges after Jonah. This time she is shouting into her earpiece: "New flier on the move. Go go go!"

I flatten myself against the alley wall and watch from the shadows as Dr. Ballinger and the "construction worker" exit the front of my building. Dr. Ballinger is making polite small talk, but the Alliance spy is listening to something in his earpiece. In the next instant, he takes off at a run, joining his partner as they thunder after Jonah. He is practically a blur of speed as he vaults over a fence, and the Alliance agents give chase.

"Maddie! We have to go!" Louisa hisses from the other end of the alley.

I know I should be running toward her, running as fast as my legs will carry me, but I just stand where I am, plastered to the rough bricks of the building. What was Jonah *thinking*? Why would he do something so crazy and so dangerous?

And then I realize: To save us. To get the attention off Louisa and me.

I feel as though the alleyway has turned to quicksand and it's trying to swallow me up.

"Come on!" Louisa urges, jerking on my elbow. "Run!"

My stomach is turning over and my head is pounding. But I do what I'm told.

I run.

We make it all the way to the L tracks before we stop to catch our breath.

"Jonah . . ." I gasp. My lungs are searing as I gulp air into them, and the muscles in my legs feel like they're on fire. "We can't leave without Jonah!"

Louisa is bent over, her hands on her knees, sucking in oxygen. She can't speak, so she simply shakes her head.

I shake mine back at her, even more vehemently. "I'm not going back to the stadium without him!"

Louisa frowns in response. After several more moments of deep breathing, she straightens up and looks at me with serious eyes. "It's not safe out here in the open, Maddie. And besides . . ." She trails off, dropping her gaze to the pavement.

"Besides what?"

But I know: we have no idea what's happened to Jonah. There's a good chance the Alliance agents caught him. Even if he managed to avoid them, he might have run right into a police officer, or got picked up by the scouts from the Phoenix School. Or maybe he met up with another gang.

I know Louisa is right. We can't just wait around here and hope that Jonah will show up.

As we climb the stairs to the El tracks and begin the long walk back, I feel tears burning behind my eyes. I struggle to hold them back, but Louisa puts her arm around my shoulders and gives me a squeeze.

"You've been brave enough for one day," she whispers. "Go ahead and cry."

That's all the encouragement I need. In the next second, the tears are spilling down my cheeks, and the frigid wind turns them icy on my skin.

Chapter 9

We arrive back at Wrigley, tired, frozen, and hungry.

"Did you find the legend?" Drew asks as soon as we appear.

"Was it on a flash drive like we thought?" Evelyn chimes in.

Numbly, I hand off the little puzzle book to Evelyn. She, Rosie, and Drew stare down at it, befuddled.

"Where's Jonah?" Alonso asks, sounding worried.

I collapse onto a hard bleacher as Louisa quietly fills everyone in on what happened: our run-in with the Daggers and the dogs, sneaking into my apartment, seeing Louisa's mom, the spies, and then Jonah running off.

"I'm sure he'll be okay," says Evelyn, giving me a hug.

"He's tough," Rosie concurs. "Don't worry."

"I can't believe you saw your mom," Ryan tells Louisa, studying her thoughtfully. Louisa nods, looking as if she wants to cry but fighting it.

Then Ryan turns to me. "You'll feel better after you eat some lunch," he says. And it's such a thoughtful and predictable thing for him to say that I actually smile.

After a quick meal of soydogs that I can barely make myself choke down, we all return to the press box. Dizzy is resting, so we're on our own for now.

Evelyn takes her place at the computer again. The encoded document looks as jumbled and unreadable as ever, but I open my book and flip through the pages.

It's like going back in time. Every page is a different game, a different challenge. The earliest pages, from when I was younger, feature simple games of Hangman. My sloppy block letters seem to teeter clumsily on the blank dashes my mother had drawn there.

"What are you looking for exactly?" Alonso asks.

I explain to my friends about how my mother and I used to write messages to each other in code and then have contests to see who could solve the puzzles faster.

About a quarter of the way through the book the games become more complicated. I remember the day my mother first taught me the word *cryptogram*. She wrote something on a fresh page in the book that to me looked like pure nonsense — letters, numbers, symbols — and told me that by the end of the week I'd be able to read it; all I had to do was discover the key. It was one of those snowy weeks in May; the blizzard conditions kept us indoors but I wasn't bored for a second. My mother had prepared a very involved scavenger hunt through which the secret of the code would be revealed to me. I'd go to brush my teeth, for example, and find a strange squiggly symbol drawn on the countertop in toothpaste. Since toothpaste begins with a *T*, I knew the squiggle represented that letter. I ran to my puzzle book and wrote it down. It went on like that for seven days, and by the end of the week, I'd compiled a complete legend with which to crack the code.

I'd sat, delightedly hunched over my puzzle book as the snow piled up outside. I matched the letters with the symbols until finally I could read that unreadable thing my mother had written. It was the Pledge of Allegiance.

Feeling a surge of hope, I flip to the page that holds that legend.

"Try this," I say to Evelyn.

She begins banging on the keys, referring to the book, and banging some more.

"Oh my gosh!" she breathes.

"Is it working?" Louisa asks.

"Yeah, I think so!" Evelyn replies excitedly. "I mean, I'm getting actual words here. *On the afternoon* . . . Maddie, quick, turn the page. . . ."

Obediently I reach over and flip to the next page in the book for Evelyn to copy. "Brilliant," she mutters. "This is positively brilliant. I'm not sure it's totally precise," she adds, typing away. "But it's close. Oh, and it ends with numbers. Hmm."

"Well, I'm sure the Hornet never expected Maddie to ever have to decipher an official Resistance document," Drew points out.

"So, Evelyn," Rosie urges, "can you make sense of it or what?"

"I think so!" says Evelyn, hitting the last key with a flourish. "Come look."

I can almost cry from relief. Now everyone rushes over to the computer, jostling for a position to better see the screen.

With the help of the legend, Evelyn has typed out:

On the afternoon of the storm, the bird knows to leave the nest.

The storm shouldn't occur.

Advise the Queen of this at the meeting at the Hive,

Where Christopher Columbus and James Monroe Meet in the New Millennium.

The utterly bizarre lines of text conclude with a

series of numbers that I can easily recognize: tomorrow's date.

"What does this all *mean*?" Ryan sputters, shaking his head.

"It's like a code within a code," Rosie says, squinting at the words. "Let's take it one thing at a time. What's up with the bird and the nest?"

I immediately think of myself — *Sparrow* — but I'm not sure that's on the right track.

"The phoenix is a mythical bird," Alonso reminds us. "So maybe the nest is the school?"

Evelyn nods excitedly. "That absolutely makes sense," she says, and Alonso blushes.

"But what about the 'afternoon of the storm'?"

"Something about the superstorms, maybe?" Louisa says. She glances at me. "Didn't you say the nurses in the Phoenix School were talking about the weather, Maddie?"

The realization is like a lightning bolt. "No, wait," I say, my heart racing. "Not 'storm,' the noun. 'Storm,' the verb. *To* storm. Another way to say *attack*."

130

Ryan claps his hands. "Now we're getting somewhere!"

"Ivan's talking about an attack!" says Rosie, her dark eyes sparkling. "On the Phoenix School."

I stand up and begin pacing the press box. It's all beginning to add up. "So what I thought the nurses were saying about something being *irresistible*," I say, working through it, "must have been them talking about the *Resistance*, *storm*ing the school!"

The implications of this information hit all of us at the same time.

"They know!" Louisa gasps. "The Phoenix School knows the Resistance is planning an attack!"

Drew nods grimly. "I think we can be pretty sure they're planning a counterstrike."

"That's horrible!" Evelyn looks furious. "The Resistance won't have a chance without the element of surprise. Someone must have tipped them off! There's a mole, or a double agent."

Rosie gives her a challenging look. "I hope you're not thinking this so-called mole is Ivan."

Evelyn shrugs.

"It's not Ivan!" Rosie plants her hands on her hips. "Absolutely not."

"You're defending him now?" asks Evelyn, confused. "The other day you nearly knocked him out."

"It was different then," Rosie snaps. "And besides, he's the one who's warning the Resistance."

"Maybe he's just making it look that way," Evelyn counters. "That's how conspiracies work!"

"Look," says Alonso, pointing to the screen. "Ivan isn't just warning them that the Phoenix faculty knows they're coming; he's advising they call off the attack. *The storm shouldn't occur.*"

Rosie shoots Evelyn a look that says, *I told you so.*

Evelyn rolls her eyes. "Well, it was possible."

Before we find ourselves in the middle of our own battle, I hold up my hands for silence. "Guys, please!"

Evelyn sighs, and Rosie relaxes, offering her an apologetic look. "Sorry. I guess I'm just anxious because Ivan said if we found the Hornet . . ."

"We'd find Wren," I finish for her. Rosie nods.

"So Ivan wanted us to get this flash drive to Maddie's mom," Louisa recaps, "to warn the Resistance not to storm the Phoenix School."

"Right," I say, pacing the press box some more. "And if we don't warn her and her soldiers in time . . ."

"There's no telling what will happen to them when they show up at the Phoenix School," Ryan finishes glumly.

"The problem is we still don't know where my mom — where the Hornet is," I say.

"There's more here," Evelyn speaks up, scrolling down the document. She checks my puzzle book, then starts typing again.

Drew leans closer to the screen to read the new words and his eyebrows lift. "According to this, the Hornet is going to meet with the Queen at some place they've coined 'the Hive.' And if those numbers just mean the date, then that meeting is tomorrow morning!"

"Who's the Queen?" Evelyn asks, but Drew doesn't look up at her.

"The Hive must be a Resistance hideout," Rosie guesses, "like a base camp or a headquarters or something."

"Maybe that line about Christopher Columbus and President James Monroe meeting in the new millennium is the clue to the location," says Evelyn.

"Whoever wrote that must have flunked American history," says Louisa, "because Columbus and Monroe lived, like, three whole centuries apart. And neither one of them was around for the new millennium."

Desperate, I pick up my puzzle book and search the pages. I am surprised when something falls out of it: a ticket stub I must have tucked in there for safekeeping. It's from the Chicago Art Institute.

"What's that?" Evelyn asks, turning and taking the stub from my hand. "Oh, the Art Institute." She gets a faraway look in her eyes. "I think I went on a field trip there once." Then her eyes widen. "Wait. The Art Institute. Hang on." She hits a few keys on the computer and a map of Chicago comes up.

"What are you doing?" I ask.

"Look!" She zooms in on the map and points to a spot. "See where South *Columbus* Drive crosses over East *Monroe* Street?"

Drew is smiling now. "At Millennium Park!"

"Right!" Evelyn exclaims. "And across the street is the Art Institute of Chicago. Well, what's left of it, anyway."

I can feel my pulse ticking faster. "My mom always said the Institute was a 'hive' of artistic genius. You guys? I'm betting the Institute is the Resistance headquarters." I squeeze Evelyn's shoulder. "You're a genius for figuring it out."

"You totally are," Rosie tells Evelyn, who beams at the compliments. Then Rosie turns to me. "But, Maddie, you were the one who figured out all the passwords and codes."

Her words please and surprise me. I know she didn't think very highly of me back at CMS, but clearly, that's changing.

Truth be told, I'm beginning to think more highly of myself, too.

"So the meeting at the Hive is tomorrow," Drew says. "And it sounds like . . . so is the planned attack."

The urgency sets in. It dawns on all of us that the only way Ivan's hard work will pay off is if we can get this message about the counterstrike to the Hornet immediately — before the Resistance storms the Phoenix School tomorrow.

"We should leave for the Art Institute now," I say, bursting to see my mother. I look at Rosie, who nods. I know she's also overwhelmed by the fact that she is now closer to finding her sister than she's been in three years.

"No — we should wait," Louisa advises, pointing outside. I look over and see a swirl of black clouds gathering overhead. The wind is picking up, and fine veins of lightning are appearing in the distance. There's no doubt that a major weather disturbance is about to occur.

Rosie wrings her hands. "This superstorm could go on all night. I need to do something with my nervous energy."

"Let's go tell Dizzy," Drew suggests. "He'll be glad to hear we've cracked the code."

"I'll go with you," says Rosie immediately, and they leave the press box.

"Hey, you guys?" Louisa looks at Evelyn, Ryan, and Alonso. "Would you mind giving Maddie and me a few minutes alone?"

Evelyn and Alonso exchange glances. "No problem," says Evelyn.

"Yeah, I think I'll go see if there are any more peanuts," says Ryan.

When they're gone, I sit down in one of the chairs, trembling. It's all been so much — going home, solving the code, knowing I might see my mother tomorrow.

Louisa sits down beside me. "Maddie, I'm so sorry," she begins, her words coming quickly and nervously. "All that awful, terrible stuff I said to you back at your apartment. It was just . . . and I was so —"

I cut her off by throwing my arms around her and giving her a huge hug. "It's okay," I assure her. "I understand. Your mom was right there, and I know how much you wanted to see her."

"But I shouldn't have said . . . I didn't mean any . . ."

"I know." I pull out of the hug to smile at her. "It's okay."

Her face registers her relief.

"Now," I say, "we should start brainstorming a plan —"

I'm interrupted by a noise from the field below:

A spine-chilling scream of pure, abject terror.

Chapter 10

Through the glass-windowed front of the press box, on the ruined baseball diamond, we see a very frightened Rosie standing face-to-face with the bristle-haired leader of the Daggers. His gang is right beside him.

"What are they doing here?" says Louisa, her voice panicked. "This is bad, Maddie."

"I don't think so," I tell her, surveying the scene. The burly guy with the white hair is standing beside the leader but he seems at ease, his rocklike shoulders relaxed, his stance almost friendly.

"But how did they know where we were?" Louisa demands.

At first, I can't even imagine. But then I notice the girl in the red vinyl ensemble is still wearing the Cubs jersey I gave her.

"I guess you could say we gave them our address," I say. "C'mon. Let's go greet our guests."

I hurry out of the press box, in case Evelyn and the boys heard Rosie's scream and decide to challenge these guys.

Louisa and I fly through the tunnel that leads to the field and come skidding to a halt between Rosie and the sooty-eyed leader.

"It's okay," I tell Rosie. I'm not used to seeing her look so scared. "They aren't here to hurt us." I'm not sure how I know this — it's just a weird sense I have.

"How do you know?" she asks in a trembling voice.

"Let's just say the Daggers and I . . . we go way back. Like all the way to this morning."

The leader's mouth turns up slightly at the corners and there is a little movement in his chest that I take for a chuckle.

The air is a lot warmer than it was just an hour ago,

and the wind is howling ominously. The sky is getting darker and darker.

"Did you come for shelter to wait out the storm?" I ask.

The leader shakes his head. "Tatz is gone."

I'm not sure who Tatz is, but Louisa realizes immediately.

"The guy with the dreadlocks and the big tattoo on his chest," she says, and the leader nods.

Only now do I realize their other member is not present.

"Some guys in uniforms grabbed him," the girl in red explains. "They had whistles around their necks, like your friend from this morning."

They are talking about Jonah, of course, and thinking of him almost makes my knees buckle with worry. "Those would be Phoenix Center scouts," I say, my voice a thread of sound.

"Our friend isn't one of them," Louisa clarifies quickly. "He was a prisoner there — that's why he has the whistle."

"I've heard of this Phoenix Center," Yellow Boots says. Her voice is panicked, and there is worry in her eyes that matches mine.

"Is he in danger?" the girl in red vinyl asks.

I decide not to sugarcoat it. "Yes," I say. "The Phoenix facility is part of the Alliance."

"Alliance!" the leader barks. "The enemy of the world. Death to the Alliance!"

No one argues with that. Even Rosie nods her agreement.

"There's a lot to explain," I say, pushing aside my fear for Jonah. "When was the last time you guys ate? We've got plenty of food if you're hungry."

Now I hear the rhythm of Dizzy's unique walk; moments later he appears at the end of the tunnel. To save him some labored steps, I immediately begin walking to meet him halfway. The Daggers, Louisa, and Rosie follow.

"Dizzy, these are the Daggers," I say. "Daggers, Dizzy."

After a brief hesitation, the leader reaches out to shake Dizzy's hand.

As Dizzy, the leader, and the bleached-blond guy begin a conversation about the state of the city, I glance at the two Dagger girls. "We've got hot water and clean towels," I say.

Their faces brighten with joy and disbelief.

"Follow me," says Louisa. "We've even got some soap and shampoo."

I notice that the girl in red vinyl has tears of gratitude in her eyes.

We treat the Daggers to soydogs with all the artificial and synthetically engineered ballpark fixings we can find. As a group, they still aren't very talkative. Like my friends and me, none of them is wearing an ID bracelet, so we don't learn their names. But a calmness has descended. We all seem to have accepted the fact that we are on the same side right now.

The storm that rages outside Wrigley is a big one; wind shrieks through the concrete corridors, while an icy rain beats an angry rhythm on the stadium seats.

"You gave me a scare before," Rosie says to the Daggers, then glances at Louisa and me. "I'm not really one to scream. But I knew you guys were preoccupied with the computers in the press box and didn't think you'd hear me otherwise."

The leader looks stunned. "You have computers here?"

"Well, if you can call them that," says Evelyn. "They're pretty prehistoric."

I notice that all of the Daggers have looks of longing on their faces and I understand immediately. "Are there people you'd like to contact?" I ask. "Family members you want to e-mail?"

The girl in red vinyl nods and the muscular one actually says, "Yes, please."

I glance at Dizzy, who smiles his consent.

"Let's go," I say, and my friends and I lead the Daggers to the press box.

The two girls and the bleached-blond guy each sit at one of the computers and Evelyn gives them a quick tutorial on using the older technology.

The leader makes the rules: he tells his friends that they can e-mail their parents only, and they are not to give their precise whereabouts. "Just tell them you're okay," he says brusquely.

I wait for him to add, *And you'll be home soon.* But he doesn't say that.

We slip off to the side of the press box in an effort to give them some privacy. Evelyn is holding the laptop we used to read the flash drive. It's quiet for a while, except for the tapping of computer keys, and the crunching sound of Ryan munching into a handful of peanuts.

Ryan gulps down the peanuts. "So what should we do tomorrow?" he asks the rest of us.

Everyone turns to me, and I realize it's up to me to lay out the plan. I take a deep breath.

"First thing tomorrow," I begin, "we have to get to the Art Institute, deliver the flash drive to my mom, and warn her that the Phoenix School is a trap."

Evelyn is looking at a map of Chicago on the computer screen. "Looks like the Institute's about six and a half miles south of here."

I turn to glance at the gang leader, who, I note sadly, has chosen not to e-mail anyone. On the one hand, I don't want him to overhear our plan, but I also realize that maybe he could be of help. "It's not exactly Dagger territory," I say to him, "but are you familiar with the route?"

He gives me a sharp little nod. "North Clark to West Lake Shore, then down North Michigan."

I notice his voice is a little dark.

Alonso picks up on it, too. "Something wrong with North Michigan?"

The muscle guy looks up from his e-mail and says in a somber voice, "Blades."

"Wonderful," says Rosie. "Gang turf." She blushes instantly, and smiles around sheepishly at our guests. "Um, no offense."

The girl with the yellow boots shrugs off the insult. "You're right to be afraid of the Blades."

I feel my heart thud in my chest. "Well, let's just hope tomorrow is the Blades' day off," I say in as cheerful a voice as I can muster.

146

Alonso is tapping his chin thoughtfully and consults Evelyn's computer. "Well, the flash drive said the meeting between the Hornet and the princess —"

"Queen," Drew corrects.

"Whatever. The meeting is in the morning. And the invasion will take place in the afternoon."

"That gives us time," says Louisa.

"We need more than time," Ryan mutters, "if we're traveling through hostile gang territory."

"We need courage," says Alonso.

"And strength," Rosie adds, "and speed."

"Weapons would be nice," says Drew.

Evelyn sighs. "Some bodyguards . . ."

Behind me, the Daggers' leader is clearing his throat. When I turn to look at him, I catch him and Yellow Boots making eye contact, as though they are sharing a thought. He then shifts his gaze to the guy with the muscles, who nods, and the girl in red vinyl blinks once, as though affirming something. Clearly they have just come to some silent decision.

"We need to sleep," the leader says suddenly.

"Oh, right." I stand up from the floor. "You guys are going to sleep here in the press box if that's okay."

He nods. Then he looks into my eyes and I wonder if he's trying to communicate something to me the way he did with his fellow gang members. If he is, I'm not getting it. Then he surprises me by placing a hand on my shoulder and giving it a quick squeeze.

"It will be all right," he says quietly, and I almost believe him.

My friends and I decide to get some sleep, too, since we'll be setting out early. That thought makes me a little light-headed, which is why I don't say much to the others as we make our way to the lockers and ready ourselves for bed.

If everything goes well and we make it to the Art Institute, I will finally, after so many, many months, be reunited with my mother. It's almost too much to comprehend.

As I rest my head on the bunched-up Cubs sweatshirt I'm using for a pillow, I try to let this amazingly happy thought relax me to sleep. But there are other thoughts getting in the way, thoughts that are not happy at all.

Like, for example, the image of all those kids from the Phoenix School. If we fail tomorrow, ultimately they will be sent to fight in the War for the very same side that kidnapped and drugged them; being forced to fight on the side of their own enemy.

And the books. All those books and the magic inside them going up in smoke.

And then there's the worst thought of all. The darkest, saddest thought, which I try to ignore, but there it is, howling and thundering in my head and my heart, as persistent and grim as the storm pounding the outer walls of the stadium.

Where is Jonah?

Jonah is gone.

It's a very long time before I even close my eyes, and much, much longer before I sleep.

We awaken to find that the Daggers are gone.

I briefly wonder where they went, or why. Perhaps

they decided to find Tatz on their own. Or they really were just seeking shelter from the storm, and didn't want to admit it. Either way, the storm has passed, and they have left. I think of the unknown Helen, off in search of her brother. Will everyone find what they are looking for?

The seven of us have a quiet meal consisting of protein bars, dried fruit, and reconstituted milk — provisions the street kids trade to Dizzy. We eat quickly, then prepare to leave.

Evelyn is slinging her backpack over one shoulder. We've decided to bring only one pack, since (hopefully) we'll be in the safekeeping of my mother by this afternoon. Tucked safely into the front pocket of the pack is the flash drive from Ivan.

She's already checked a thousand times to be sure it's still there.

"Where else would it be?" Rosie huffs, rolling her eyes. But then she smiles at Evelyn and *she* checks the pocket to make sure we have the walkie-talkie cell phones. We all understand how crucial this mission is and no one is about to take it lightly.

As we make our way to the stadium exit, everyone is feeling jittery and excited and a little bit scared. We take a few minutes to go over the route with Dizzy. We've got a walk of about six miles, through hostile territory, and Dizzy checks Alonso's knee and Drew's shoulder.

"I'm good," Alonso assures him. "Feels great."

"Me, too," says Drew. "Doesn't hurt at all."

I wonder if they're telling the truth. I know they'll go through with this mission even if they are in the worst pain ever, so I just hope they feel as up to snuff as they're saying.

Dizzy tells us to keep to the middle of the road and not to wander into any alleyways or side streets.

"Sounds like good advice to me," mumbles Evelyn.

Now Dizzy hands a hefty aluminum baseball bat to Ryan. "Just in case," he says.

"In case what?" quips Ryan, grinning his goofy grin.

151

"In case we feel like stopping along the way to shag some fly balls?"

"Yeah." Dizzy smiles. "In case you do."

But we all know what the bat is "in case" of: an unexpected run-in with the Blades.

As the others pass through the rusted turnstile to the exit, Dizzy motions to me. "Give my best to your mother," he says in a voice thick with emotion.

"You can do it yourself when you see her," I tell him, trying to sound confident. "And once we get your leg fixed up, I'm sure you'll be joining her in action."

He swallows, then nods, but can't seem to manage a smile.

"I'll tell her you took real good care of us," I say, but for some reason it comes out in a whisper.

I catch up to the others on the sidewalk, where they are all staring up at the big red sign of the stadium. Last night's storm did even more damage to it. The wind destroyed several of the remaining letters, so now all that's left is the word *home*.

"Appropriate," says Rosie.

Evelyn, even without her compass, is able to point the way. "North Clark to West Lake Shore to North Michigan," she declares.

"Let's go," says Drew, clapping his hands.

Louisa high-steps to the front of the group and gives us a mischievous smile. I know she's trying to lighten the mood — to keep us from falling into the brink of fear.

"You heard the guy," she barks, in a passable impression of a tough-as-nails drill sergeant. "Everybody! Forward . . . *march!*"

What else can we do? We march.

Chapter 11

When Louisa, Jonah, and I went to my apartment, we thought three kids on the streets would look less conspicuous at an early hour. This time, we've decided to start our trek so that it coincides with the school and factory commute. Since it's all seven of us now, Rosie thought that blending in with the crowd, at least for part of the walk, would be safer. A bunch of thirteen-year-olds wandering the street on a school day would surely attract the attention of the cops.

Or the Alliance.

As we walk, jostled by the stone-faced masses in their gritty work clothes, I try to imagine what this part of the city must have been like, back when there were handsome skyscrapers lining these streets. Then, I imagine, the buildings were filled with offices and businesses run by men and women earning their livings in a peaceful world.

Now the workforce is made up mostly of factory employees, who dress in heavy jumpsuits supplied by the munitions manufacturers they work for. The office buildings and high-rise condominiums that once stood here have been either demolished or so severely neglected that they're falling down on their own. And the superstorms have wreaked havoc. There are chunks of concrete missing from the sidewalks, and the smell of burning garbage assaults us around every corner.

"Look at that," says Louisa in a low voice.

I turn in the direction she's pointing and I can't believe what I am seeing. It is a tidy line of schoolchildren, much younger than we are, walking to school. They are all dressed in perfectly matching uniforms: plaid jumpers on the girls, crisp khaki trousers and plaid neckties for the boys. They are being guided by an uppity-looking headmaster, who walks in front of them.

These are probably the great-grandchildren of the families from the Lincoln Park area. Before the world went nuts, Lincoln Park was one of the most sought-after neighborhoods in Chicago.

"Are they seriously on a *leash*?" Evelyn whispers.

And now I realize why Louisa pointed them out to me. The kids are tethered together by a long chain. Each kid has a steel cuff loosely encircling his or her right ankle, and the cuffs are connected by the chain, which ends where it is linked to a cuff on the headmaster's wrist. The shiny metallic chain glints in the pale sunlight.

I happen to glance at Drew, and he's stark pale, looking like he might pass out. I know it's not his shoulder, though. It's the sight of these kids, chained together like prisoners. It's horrifying, but of course it's a safety precaution. Nowadays, the children of the truly wealthy are always in danger of being kidnapped for ransom, and that's just by regular, run-of-the-mill local criminals. There's also the threat of the Alliance.

And now I understand. This is the real reason my

friends' parents sent them to CMS. The condition of the city, the filth and lack of clean water and fresh air, was only part of it. It hadn't really registered before, but seeing these children chained together like prisoners hammers it home. The threat is incredibly real.

As I found out, the hard way. My parents aren't rich by any means, but my mother is the Hornet, and that put me in the most danger of all.

Now one little girl in the lineup turns to look at me. She's probably no more than seven, and she's adorable. Button nose, perfect golden curls, and cobalt blue eyes. The pressed pleats of her school jumper flounce lightly as she walks in time with her classmates.

I smile at her.

She sticks her tongue out at me.

"Wow," says Ryan. "I hope I never get rich enough that my kids have to be shackled."

Everyone agrees with him, and we keep walking.

As the factory crowd begins to thin, the street goes quiet. As Dizzy advised, we walk down the middle of the broad main thoroughfare to avoid being ambushed from doorways and alleys. There are no cars in sight, naturally — we've gotten all too used to that.

We've been walking for a few miles, when Drew points to something in the distance.

"Pop quiz," he says. "Anybody know what that building is — well, used to be — called?"

Quite a ways off, looming several stories above the tallest building in view, is the toothy skeleton of what once was an enormous tower made of glass and steel.

"It was the Sears Tower," answers Evelyn. "And then they changed the name to Willis. At one time, it was the tallest building in the whole wide world."

We all know the story of this amazing landmark. It stood here overlooking Lake Michigan and the Chicago River and the elegant city skyline for decades until a superstorm swept through the city last year and sliced it in half. Once 110 stories high, it's been chopped down to a mere fifty. Unfortunately, on its way down, it took out a lot of the neighboring buildings with it, leaving a gaping wound in the city.

My mother cried for a week.

So did every other grown-up in Chicago.

The cleanup from that disaster took six whole months, with bulldozers scooping up the rubble and dumping it into the river, which no one complained about since it was already so polluted it was little more than sludge, anyway.

"I was there once," Drew tells us. "On the Skydeck, for the farewell bash. The view was the coolest thing I'd ever seen."

"Really?" I ask, shocked. The Skydeck was the name of the observation deck on the 103rd floor of the Willis Tower, but it was closed to visitors two years ago, when the global weather center determined that the force of the earth's winds had increased severely and permanently. There was a big farewell ceremony to commemorate the doors being sealed shut forever. The event was invitation only, and was attended by the wealthiest, most important citizens of Chicago as well as a bunch of high-level politicians from all over.

I am about to ask Drew how he managed to score such an exclusive ticket, but Evelyn has suddenly grabbed my arm and is dragging me as she runs after Ryan. Alonso has taken hold of Drew's shirt with one hand and Rosie's arm with the other and he's running, too. Louisa is hot on their heels.

The next thing I know the seven of us are crouched behind a rusted Dumpster.

My heart is slamming against my chest as I turn to Evelyn. "What's wrong? Who are we hiding from?"

I expect to hear her say *Blades.*

She doesn't, but what she says is just as troubling.

"The police."

If I hadn't been gazing off into the distance, looking at the rubble-formerly-known-as-the-Sears-Tower, I would have seen them coming.

The police car is screeching to a halt in the middle of the street. An ad for Liquid Heat Rub, a muscle-soothing pain ointment, is splashed across the hood; the painted flames almost make it look as though the police car is on fire. The siren is silent, but the blue lights are flashing. Two officers jump out; one has drawn his gun.

This doesn't make sense. Even if they'd seen us — seven kids wandering through a rough section of town — there's still no need for this kind of reaction. They couldn't have possibly known that we weren't wearing ID bracelets. So what's all the fuss about?

I get my answer in the next second, when I peek out from around the side of the Dumpster and see three wild-eyed teenage boys come bolting out of an alley across the street.

Blades, for sure. They look far more terrifying than the Daggers. All three of them have tattooed faces and they have shaved their heads completely. The police holler for them to freeze, and a second police car skids into view, this one with its siren wailing.

Beside me, Evelyn is shaking uncontrollably. Louisa, Rosie, Alonso, and Drew have gone pale, and Ryan is holding on to the aluminum bat for dear life.

I can no longer see the action, but I hear the sound of the gang members running away. Then there is an ear-splitting squeal from the police car's loudspeaker, followed by the staticky, amplified voice of an officer: "They're heading west down Madison."

One car revs its engine and takes off with its tires smoking. We can hear the siren blaring, then fading, as the car speeds farther away in pursuit of the gang.

We wait for the other car to follow.

After what seems like forever, it finally does. But we still aren't alone. There are voices approaching. They are young-sounding, with a mean, clipped quality.

I piece the scenario together quickly — the other Blade members led the cops away while these two were hiding nearby.

"Where are they?" asks one.

"They're hiding behind that garbage thing."

They, of course, meaning . . . us. The Blades saw us take cover behind the Dumpster!

"What we gonna do with 'em?" the first voice wonders.

162

"Sell 'em," says the second. "Their families'll pay lots for 'em to come home in one piece."

I think I might throw up.

The footsteps thud closer and when I open my eyes, I see two Blades — much scarier than the three who ran from the cops — standing at each corner of the Dumpster, giving us nowhere to run.

One of them grabs Drew, tugging him out from behind the Dumpster by his injured shoulder. Drew lets out a cry of pain as the second one takes hold of my wrist and pulls me out. I struggle, but this guy outweighs me by about fifty pounds.

The others clamber out frantically from behind the Dumpster.

"Let her go!" Louisa screams, flinging herself at the gang member who's tugging on my wrist. Evelyn follows her, swinging her backpack like a weapon, but of course it does nothing. The Blade doesn't budge.

Rosie is kicking at the one who's got Drew in a head-lock; Alonso has jumped onto his back, and is pounding on him for all he's worth. Ryan is holding the bat, ready to swing, but he's not sure whom to go after first.

And then we hear a whistle. Three blasts: one short, two more short, one long.

I hear the barking almost instantly.

So do the Blades. The one holding my wrist is startled enough to loosen his grip, just long enough for me to break free. Then the dogs come stampeding into the alleyway. They charge toward the Blades. The air is filled with the bloodcurdling snarls and growls of the Daggers' pets. And speaking of which . . .

The Daggers have arrived and they are forming a solid line, looking ferocious and determined. The dogs do not attack, but kneel by their masters, simply waiting for their command.

I look at the faces of the Daggers, feeling a rush of gratitude. They must have heard Evelyn last night, saying she wished we had bodyguards. They decided to follow us on our journey, to protect us, and they brought their pets as well. Yellow Boots extends her hand to Ryan, who immediately tosses her the aluminum bat.

The Blades look a little less terrifying, knowing that they are outnumbered. In fact, they themselves look scared.

The muscular Dagger motions with his head for us to step away from the Blades. We do, moving quickly until we are at what seems a safe distance, with the Daggers and their dogs between us and our enemies.

The leader looks at me and in a voice that does not allow for discussion, he orders, "Run."

In the next heartbeat, my friends and I are running as fast as we can, away from the Blades and the Daggers.

"Find Tatz!" Yellow Boots calls after us. "Please!"

I glance over my shoulder and am relieved to see that the Blades have taken off in the opposite direction. The Daggers and dogs do not follow them, and I'm glad. They've done what they came to do. There is no need for them to fight these guys.

"I guess you never know where help will come from," Rosie mutters as we run, our feet pounding the pavement, and I silently agree, too nervous and scared to speak.

My friends and I don't stop running until we find ourselves at the corner of East Monroe and North Michigan.

There, less than twenty yards away, is the Art Institute. Out of breath, we make our way toward the main entrance.

It's a heartbreaking thing to see.

The once beautifully constructed Art Institute is now a sad, forgotten place. With its two levels of tall arches spanning the main entrance, it used to look like something that survived since the days of ancient Rome. Now the arches are crumbling, and the outer walls are charred, ingrained with black soot from the fire.

The front door is locked — of course. The Resistance wouldn't be meeting in a building that anyone could stroll into. I pound on the door, imagining — what? That my mother would appear and open it? If we're right and the Resistance is meeting here, then they must be holed up somewhere deep inside the museum.

"Let's go around to the side," Alonso suggests. When we do, we find a loose windowpane, probably shaken up and forgotten in the destruction. Together, Rosie and Ryan manage to force it all the way open, and one by one, we each slide inside, trying to land soundlessly in our sneakers.

I look around, my blood roaring in my ears. *We're inside.*

The Grand Staircase, which splits at a center landing and goes off in four directions, had always reminded me of something from a fairy-tale castle. When I was small, I would climb it, holding the smooth, polished banister. Now the banister is gone; the once-pristine marble steps are chipped, and in some places broken in large chunks. The whole place still reeks of dirty smoke, and a heavy coating of dust and ash covers everything.

"The museum is huge," Louisa points out. "The Hornet could be anywhere."

"Should we spread out?" asks Evelyn. "It would be faster."

I nod. "Good idea."

We split into groups — Ryan and Rosie go up to the second level, Louisa and Alonso head right, toward the Ryerson and Burnham libraries, and Drew, Evelyn, and I go straight, past the Grand Staircase and through the Alsdorf Galleries.

The glass cases that once protected priceless statues and carvings are shattered and the smaller artifacts were stolen by looters long ago. But there is still one figure. It sits as proudly and peacefully as ever in the middle of the long gallery, because it is far too large and way too heavy for anyone to steal.

In spite of the urgency of our mission, we can't help but pause to admire it.

"Buddha Seated in Meditation," Drew reads aloud from the plaque that remains.

"He's smiling," Evelyn observes.

"He's glad we're here," I say.

We're about to keep moving when we hear a voice.

"Halt immediately!"

Drew, Evelyn, and I turn to see a pair of enormous soldiers in gray fatigues striding toward us from the far end of the gallery.

Drew gives me a panicked look. "We can just tell

them you're the Hornet's daughter," he suggests frantically. "Maybe they'll take us to her."

"Maybe," I say quickly. "But what if they decide to hold us somewhere while they check out our stories? By the time they confirm our identities, the Resistance soldiers could be halfway to the Phoenix School."

"Right," Evelyn agrees, bouncing anxiously on the balls of her feet as the guards close the gap. "So . . . we run?"

"We run!"

Our sneakers squeak on the ash-coated floor as we take off through the gallery. The guards give chase. One of them barks into a wristband radio: "Intruders in the Alsdorf sector. In pursuit."

We skid to a halt in a long corridor. "Left!" I cry.

Around that corner, we come to the entrance to the Rubloff Auditorium. We can hear the guards' boots pounding closer. With only seconds to spare, we duck breathlessly into the theater and flatten ourselves against the interior wall; our pursuers thunder past the main door. Not until the sound of their running footsteps fades into the distance do I relax slightly and look around the auditorium. The mustard-colored upholstery on the seats is tattered and singed. Half of the mezzanine section has collapsed.

But miraculously the stage is still standing. The enormous room is dim except for a small pool of light in the center of the stage that is coming from a battery-operated lantern on a table. The glow illuminates the table and two women leaning over it, examining some kind of map or document.

One of them, dressed in army boots and gray fatigues, appears to be a young soldier.

And the other one is my mother.

Chapter 12

I open my mouth to call out *Mom*, the word I haven't been able to say since she went away so many months ago. But I can't seem to find my voice.

So I begin to move, slowly at first, my eyes fixed on her up on that stage. I step over pieces of broken auditorium seats and chunks of crumbling plaster. With every step, my heart seems to thud harder and harder in my chest, and suddenly, I'm running faster than I ever have, faster than I ran from the guards.

I hop onto the stage, startling my mother and the soldier.

I can tell that, at first, my mother can't believe it's

me. She shakes her head, as though she fears she's dreaming.

I smile at her.

And when she understands that I am not a dream or a hallucination or a hologram or anything else but her daughter, she opens her arms and I hurl myself into them, across the stage, across the months, across the loneliness and the fear and the secrets.

"Maddie!" she whispers into my hair. "What are you doing here?"

Still, I can't talk. All I can do is burrow my face into her shoulder, breathing her in, and feeling her arms around me.

"Maddie," she says again. "It's so good to see you."

Her voice sweeps over me like a cool breeze on a hot day.

The young soldier steps off the stage, as if to give us privacy. Mom squeezes me tight. Then I'm suddenly aware of someone else joining us on the stage. Over my mother's shoulder I see a woman appear from behind the shredded curtains that shield the stage's wings. This woman isn't wearing the army boots and gray fatigues of the Resistance, though; she's dressed in a neat pantsuit and her dark hair is twisted up in a bun.

It only takes me a moment to recognize who she is.

Her name is Carolyn Andrews Kim.

And she happens to be the President of the United States of America.

The Queen. That's what Ivan's message must have meant.

As amazing as that is, right now, all I can focus on is my mother. Finally, I open my mouth to speak to her.

"Mom! Hey, Mom!"

But it's not my voice that rings through the auditorium.

It's Drew's.

I turn to see him bolting down the theater aisle just as I had. Evelyn is on his heels and there is a look of utter disbelief on her face.

President Kim is squinting into the shadows of the auditorium. Then the voice I've heard speaking to the world over the NewsServ a million times is calling, "Drew? Honey, is that you?"

Drew springs up onto the stage and runs to embrace the *other* most important woman in the country . . . who apparently just happens to be *his* mother.

I watch in shock as President Kim hugs Drew. Then I turn to my mother and I almost start laughing. She's staring back at me with an expression that says: *How do you know President Kim's son?*

All I can think to say is: *We have a lot of catching up to do.* But before I can, we hear a commotion near the theater entrance. We all turn to see Louisa, Ryan, Rosie, and Alonso being hauled into the auditorium by three guards.

My mother looks at me questioningly; I nod, and she waves to the guards to bring my friends to the stage. Naturally, they recognize instantly that the woman ruffling Drew's hair is the commander in chief. Louisa and

Alonso stare in disbelief. Rosie's mouth is hanging open from absolute shock. Ryan shoots Drew a sideways glance, and says what every one of us is thinking:

"Dude. You've *gotta* be kidding me."

"Your mother is the *President* of the *United States*?" Evelyn shrieks in a whisper.

Drew's eyes twinkle with mischief. "So it would seem."

"Oh!" Louisa flings her arms wide. "And you didn't think that was worth *mentioning*?!"

"I didn't want to freak everyone out," he says, serious now. "And I didn't want to be treated differently than the others."

I don't know if I want to sock him in the jaw for concealing such a major piece of information, or hug him for being so modest, and for not pulling rank. Instead, I just continue holding tight to my own mom, who is now looking at my best friend.

"Louisa? I don't understand!" my mother says. She pulls Louisa into our hug and squeezes her. "You're here, too? How did you find us?"

President Kim is looking at Drew like any ordinary mother would look at her son, with love in her eyes. "You're supposed to be at Country Manor, where it's safe," she says. "What happened?"

"It's complicated," Drew answers, in what is perhaps the understatement of the century.

Now I feel Louisa tugging on my sleeve. "Hey . . . look."

I follow her gaze to where Rosie is standing near the edge of the stage, fidgeting like crazy.

"Mom," I say, motioning to Rosie. "See that girl over there? Her name is Rosie. She's looking for her sister. Wren Chavez. Do you know where she is?"

"As a matter of fact, I do." My mom presses a button on the wristband communication device she's wearing. Two seconds later, a girl with a gleaming black ponytail and dark eyes comes striding out from the backstage area.

I'd know her anywhere. In fact, if it weren't for the gray camouflage pants, the army boots, and the fact that she stands about five foot eight, I'd have mistaken her for Rosie.

My mother smiles at the girl and nods toward the edge of the stage at the same exact moment that Rosie turns to look in our direction.

When the sisters spot each other, I feel my eyes fill with tears.

Rosie and Wren run to each other, and then Rosie is caught up in her older sister's arms. Wren swings Rosie around in a circle, as they laugh and cry at the same time.

"I missed you so much," says Rosie, with tears streaming down her cheeks.

"Oh, I missed you, too, *hermanita*," says Wren. "I'm so sorry I couldn't tell you where I was. But it seems you found me, anyway. What are you doing here?"

"Well, it's kind of a long story." Rosie sniffles as Wren puts her back down on her feet. "How much time have you got?"

Not much, I realize, suddenly remembering why we've come here.

I hold out my hand to Evelyn, who immediately hands me the flash drive. I turn to my mother.

"Ivan Franks asked us to deliver this to you," I explain, and my mother's eyes — so like my own in color and shape — widen.

At the mention of Ivan's name, Wren lets out a small gasp. "You saw Ivan?" she whispers, color rushing into her face. "Is he okay?"

I swallow hard. The last I saw of Ivan, he was being caught by scouts while we drove off in the getaway van.

"He's strong," Rosie tells her sister. "I think he'll be fine. He's at the Phoenix School."

This reminds me to turn back to my mom. "You have to call off today's attack on the Phoenix School!" I say quickly. "We read it on the flash drive — it's a trap!"

My mom (who's used to me asking for second helpings of reconstituted chocolate-substitute pudding and complaining about homework) is taken aback.

"Maddie, how do you know about the Phoenix School?" she asks. She takes the flash drive from my hand. "And how on earth did you decipher what was on here?"

My friends and I exchange glances. There *isn't* much time, but we do have to explain. So, we ask my mom,

Drew's mom, and Wren to join us off the stage, on seats in the auditorium. And, talking together, we catch them up.

Louisa starts, speaking softly about what happened at CMS. Then Rosie joins in, explaining how we ran off. When she gets to this part, my mom's eyes widen again and she looks like she wants to scold me. But then Alonso is explaining about the woods, and then we get up to the part when I was taken.

At this point, my mom's mouth forms a thin, determined line that I know so well.

"You were *at* the Phoenix Center?" she says, her voice barely above a whisper. She rests her hand against my cheek, as if she can't believe I made it out in one piece.

I nod, not sure I believe it, either.

Squeezing my hand, Evelyn picks up the rest of the story, recounting how the group made its way closer to Chicago and figured out how to find me. Alonso explains about Wrigley Field and Dizzy, causing Wren to exclaim, "You met *Dean*?" Finally, I finish up by describing our dangerous trek back to our apartment — my mom goes

179

pale at this — and then finding the puzzle book, and deciphering the code. At this, Mom brightens a bit.

"Everything you did," she says firmly, looking first at me and then the others, "was highly dangerous and ill-advised. But," she adds, her eyes coming to rest on me, "I must commend you on your astonishing acts of bravery."

My friends and I look at one another, and I can hear Alonso whisper to Ryan, "Dude. The Hornet thinks we rock."

Mom speaks rapidly into her wristband again, asking a soldier to come out with her tablet. When the young soldier returns bearing Mom's sleek tablet computer, I think of Dad, and ask worriedly about him.

"He's fine," Mom assures me, inserting the flash drive into the tablet. "He's out in the suburbs of Chicago today, working on wiring a new spot for the Resistance to hide out in — we're always changing locations, for security purposes." Mom glances at me, and her eyes well up. "I can't wait to tell him you're here."

I can't wait to see my father again, too — to have my family all back together.

With a nod of her head, Wren urges Mom to enter the flash drive into her tablet. It's the kind of firm, capable motion that I can see Rosie making. The sisters are so similar I can't help but smile, despite our situation.

Mom inserts the flash drive, and her fingers fly over the keys as she types in the password *freedom* and accesses the document. She reads it quickly, instantly absorbing what it took us forever to get. She also points out that there are other documents on the flash drive — we were too distracted to even notice those — with more details about the Phoenix School.

"Okay," she says decisively, looking from Wren to the young soldier. "They're definitely going to counterstrike. We're going to call off the mission for now. Postpone it."

I have a reckless thought that I can't keep to myself. "Mom," I say boldly. "Maybe there's a way you can still go today. Counterstrike their counterstrike."

"We will," my mother says. "Eventually. But it's just too risky to try today. They know we're aware of them, and that puts a very dangerous spin on things."

But I keep going. "You don't understand what that

place is like," I say heatedly. "The longer those kids stay drugged and brainwashed, the more difficult it's going to be to get them back to reality." I look at Louisa, Rosie, and Evelyn. "I would have stayed if it weren't for my friends . . . and who knows what would have happened."

A flash of concern darkens my mom's eyes. I realize that, suddenly, this mission has hit very close to home for her.

"Let me think about it," she tells me. "We'll see."

Now, when other mothers say "we'll see" it's pretty certain that the answer is going to be "no."

But as it turns out, when your mother is the commander of a high-powered, undercover rebel army, what "we'll see" really means is: *Let me talk to my military advisors, organize an infiltration sequence, and prepare a viable assault strategy.*

Command Central is located down the hall from the Rubloff Auditorium in a huge area called the Stock Exchange Trading Room. It once featured the actual stenciled decorations and art glass of the historic Chicago Stock Exchange, but the fire severely damaged the space. Now it is a secret military outpost, the base of operations for the Resistance forces.

My mother suggested summoning vehicles to take President Kim and the rest of us to a safe house but we all flat-out refused. My mom argued for only a minute. I suppose there was something in our eyes, some steely resolve in our voices, that told her this was one battle even the Hornet couldn't win.

Now she and her team are struggling to come up with a way to infiltrate the Phoenix Center stronghold to apprehend the Alliance faculty.

My friends and I are seated on wooden chairs in the corner of the huge space, watching in awe as the Hornet and her soldiers do their thing. There are maps spread out on folding tables, and dry-erase boards already covered with hand-drawn diagrams and possible strategic procedures. There's a section being guarded by two powerful-looking soldiers that contains an arsenal of weapons. And there is a table piled high with protein bars and energy drinks.

So far, Ryan is the only one of us who could bring himself to eat.

"How can you think about food at a time like this?" snaps Rosie.

"Soldiers need their strength," he says.

I realize that by being in this room, by doing what we've done, we are like soldiers now. Two years ahead of schedule. I look at the young Resistance soldiers in the room, and think of Ivan, and Dizzy. Then my thoughts jump to Jonah, out there alone, and I feel a pang of missing him. It doesn't seem fair that I'm reunited with my mother, and he's all alone.

Louisa, doing her mind-reading thing again, pats my arm. "I think Jonah's okay," she tells me softly. "He's been out on his own before. He's like Helen, and her brother, Troy."

I think of Helen, that mysterious stranger who made such a huge contribution to my own rescue. I wonder if she's found Troy.

Helen and Troy. There's something about those names that strikes a chord in me. For some reason, I conjure up the image of an old book.

The memory comes back slowly — there was a book at the Phoenix School, one I was supposed to toss into the fire. But the size and weight of it had intrigued me, and I just had to look inside. The book was called *The Odyssey*, an epic poem translated from ancient Greek, and it included a story about a beautiful girl named Helen, who was stolen from her husband and taken to the city of Troy. Helen and Troy — such a funny coincidence. I wonder if their parents had loved *The Odyssey*.

I'm gnawing on my lower lip and my eyebrows are scrunched down as I recall the few pages I managed to read before a Phoenix supervisor yelled at me to throw the book into the flames. The more I remember, the more the ideas start to swirl in my mind; I can feel the beginning of a plan tingling in the back of my brain.

"Uh-oh," says Louisa. "I know that look. It was the look she had just before she made me walk across an ironing board."

185

But I'm deep into remembering the story now, especially the part about how when the soldiers came to rescue Helen, they got into the city of Troy by hiding inside a giant horse. I glance over to the protein bars on the table.

Suddenly, I know exactly how we're going to get into the Phoenix Center.

Chapter 13

I run across the dulled wood floor directly to my mother. My friends are right behind me.

"What is it, Maddie?" my mother asks. She's staring at a blueprint of the Harold Washington Library, which is now the Phoenix School.

"Even the bad guys have to eat!" I blurt.

My mother looks at me strangely for a second, then places her hand on my forehead to feel for a fever.

"Mom, I'm not sick! I have a plan!" I take a deep breath and explain. "The Phoenix School gets its food — the drugged stuff for the students and the clean stuff for the teachers — from NutriCorp."

"NutriCorp!" says Ryan. "The world's foremost suppliers of tofu chili and Cheezy-Wizard!"

"A delivery truck arrives every day at three o'clock," I tell my mother, recalling what Jonah had said about his unloading chore. "All we have to do is get ahold of the truck on its way to the school. Then we take all the food out of the boxes, and our *soldiers* can get inside the boxes instead. We can dress some other soldiers as the deliverymen. They'll carry the soldiers into the building totally unnoticed."

My mother is beaming with pride. "Maddie . . . that's brilliant." Her smile fades slightly. "But there's one problem. They already have a plan in place for our arrival. It will definitely be in our favor to attack from inside instead of approaching from the perimeter, but there's still a chance that even if we catch them unawares, they'll be prepared enough to fight back."

"Not if they're in lockdown," I say triumphantly.

"Lockdown," echoes Wren. "Ivan included information about the lockdown process on the flash drive."

"That's because they take it very seriously," I say. "They have tons of drills, practicing the procedure. If a

lockdown alarm sounds, every individual in the school —
students *and* teachers — *must* report immediately to their
assigned stations. The students gather in an auditorium
on the lower level, with senior scouts to oversee them.
The teachers and administrators gather in this place
called the Chicago Authors Room on the seventh floor.
They won't have time to collect weapons or anything
before they report there. And once they're all inside, the
doors and windows are wired to lock automatically."

"Wow," says Drew, with a wry grin. "That's perfect.
They'll be trapping themselves!"

"Right!" I say. "And *that's* when the soldiers will burst
out of the NutriCorp boxes and capture them all at once."

"Wait a minute," says Evelyn. "Who's going to sound
the lockdown alarm?"

"Someone who knows all the ins and outs of the
school. Someone," I say, throwing my shoulders back.
"Like me."

It takes ten solid minutes of arguing, reasoning, and
insisting before my mom finally agrees to let me go back

to the Phoenix Center. She doesn't like the idea all that much, but she understands that it's the only way this plan will work.

A regiment of Resistance soldiers will be hidden in boxes and metal drum containers to be delivered to the Phoenix School. I will be entering the school the same way, but my role in this mission is to exit my box first, and sound the alarm.

My mother, Wren, and I are poring over the library blueprints. My friends are looking on, enthralled.

"There," I say, pointing to a room on the plan. "That's where the alarm is activated. The Superior's office."

"Miss Castle," says Louisa distastefully.

"The lady with the killer pinkie," grumbles Ryan.

"If I can get into that office, all I have to do is pull the alarm and the whole faculty go straight to the Chicago Authors Room. Once they're locked inside, I can alert the soldiers in the boxes and they can do the rest."

I do my best not to sound scared, but I will admit

that I am thoroughly terrified. The fires in the boiler room, the cadets keeping their eyes on you, the wicked faculty — not exactly the kinds of things anyone in their right mind would choose to relive.

The Madeleine Frye who got on the bus to CMS would have never dreamed of such a thing.

But I have to do it. Not only for the good of the country but also for all the kids who are still being held there.

"A soldier is never sent into enemy territory alone," my mother says.

Wren nods. "Maddie, you're going to need a partner, someone to have your back."

The words are barely out of her mouth, but six hands have already shot into the air.

If there's one thing we've learned on this journey, it's that all of my friends have qualities or skills that would make them useful in this situation. In a perfect world, we could all go, because what really makes our abilities worthwhile is how they all work together.

But this is definitely not a perfect world, so I find myself having to choose.

My gut instinct is to choose Louisa. She's been with me through everything from losing my first tooth to breaking into my own apartment. But there's a risk. She was at the Phoenix School for my rescue, as were Ryan, Evelyn, and Rosie. It's possible that one of the scouts will recognize them.

There's a risk that I'll be recognized, too, but Evelyn's already come up with an idea for that.

I consider taking Drew, but I know how hard it's going to be to drag myself away from my mom now that I've found her, so I don't really want to ask him to leave his.

"Alonso," I say. "I pick Alonso." He's quick-thinking, and brave.

Everyone opens their mouths at once, and I'm prepared for a huge argument. But Wren defuses the situation by announcing that there will be plenty of responsibilities for all of them here at Command Central.

"Now," says Wren. "You must all choose your Resistance code names. It will be easier for you to communicate this way during the mission. They should be short and easy to remember." She gives us a moment to think, then walks down the line, pointing to each of us in turn as we call out our chosen code names.

"Water Bug," says Louisa.

"Chowhound," says Ryan.

"Conspirator," says Evelyn.

"Fly Boy," says Alonso. "No, wait. Dictionary Dude."

"I'm gonna go with Little Prez," says Drew, and his mom rolls her eyes.

"*Hermanita*," says Rosie.

Now it's my turn. "I think I'll keep the code name I've always had," I say. "Sparrow."

"Excellent," says President Kim.

"All of you go have some food," my mother instructs. "You're soldiers now and you have to keep up your strength."

Ryan gives us a look. "Told ya." Then he hurries off

to help himself to another protein bar and some dehydrated fruit rations.

But I'm not hungry.

After all, I'm going back to the Phoenix School. And that would kill anyone's appetite.

It's two thirty and my mother has dispatched a unit to take over the NutriCorp truck, which has been spotted entering the city limits by one of her reconnaissance soldiers.

Meanwhile, Louisa, Evelyn, and Rosie get busy on my "makeover."

I shake my hair out of its signature messy bun and follow them into the nearest ladies' room.

Desperate times call for desperate haircuts.

So, forty-five minutes later, Louisa, Evelyn, Rosie, and I emerge. My three personal stylists shield me from the boys, in preparation for the unveiling.

"Ta-da!" cries Evelyn.

With great drama, they sweep their arms in my direction and step aside, revealing my new look.

"What do you think?" I ask. The back of my neck feels cold.

Drew, Alonso, and Ryan are staring at me, their mouths hanging open, their eyes round.

"Maddie?" says Alonso. "Is that really you?"

"Your hair . . ." says Drew.

Louisa holds up a pair of scissors. "I cut it!" she announces proudly.

"Do you like it?" I ruffle the feathery sweep of layers that now frame my face. I have bangs for the first time in my life. "Be honest."

"Well, sure we like it," says Ryan. "It's just so . . . short!"

"And so . . . *blond*!" Alonso adds.

"Yeah," says Drew. "How'd that happen?"

"I dyed it for her," says Evelyn. "I borrowed some chemicals from those guys." She motions with her chin toward the soldiers guarding the weapons reserve.

"Chemicals?" Ryan repeats, horrified. "Like . . . nerve gas?"

"No, you knucklehead," Rosie says. "We wouldn't use nerve gas on Maddie's head! We used hydrogen peroxide. From their medical kit."

Ryan visibly relaxes at that revelation.

Wren approaches us, carrying a pair of thick-rimmed glasses. "Put these on," she says. "They're not prescription. They're just magnifiers, which we use to read maps and other small printed documents."

I slip the glasses onto the bridge of my nose, and everything increases in size by about a zillion percent. I wobble slightly on my feet.

"You'll get used to it in a few minutes," says Wren. She smiles at Rosie and the others. "You girls did a great job. I would have never recognized her."

"Let's hope the same is true for the Alliance," I say. I'm pretty sure this disguise is foolproof. As far as they know, Madeleine Frye is a curly-haired brunette with 20/20 vision, not a short-haired blonde with eyeglasses.

Now my mother appears to tell us that the soldiers have returned with the truck and the empty NutriCorp boxes. She smiles at my new appearance. "Cute." Then she gives me a kiss on the forehead. "Be careful, Sparrow," she says, with a catch in her voice. "You, too, Alonso. I mean, Dictionary Dude."

"Good luck," says President Kim.

The Hornet and President Kim go off to consult with the soldiers who will be posing as deliverymen. Fear swells in me, threatening to steal all my breath. Part of me wants to run after my mom and beg her to order me to stay here, but I don't.

Doing what you have to do, even when you're scared to death. That's what's called for now.

Wren leads all seven of us out to the NutriCorp truck, which will be our Trojan horse. I can feel my heart pounding double time.

Wren fits Alonso and me with wristband communicators. She gives Alonso a salute, then hugs me and whispers, "Thanks for being such a good friend to my sister."

I smile, remembering the rocky start Rosie and I had back at CMS. "My pleasure" is all I say.

Wren wishes us luck, then leaves.

"This is so unfair," says Rosie, folding her arms stubbornly across her chest. "I can't believe I have to wait here. I mean, I should be going. My sister is a major Resistance operative."

"So?" Ryan gives her a look. "What's that got to do with anything?"

"Maybe military smarts runs in families," says Rosie. "Maybe courage is hereditary."

Evelyn rolls her eyes. "Well, if family ties matter so much, wouldn't you think Drew should be going in? I mean, he's the Commander in Chief Junior."

"Oh, please." Rosie is so agitated she speaks without thinking. "Drew's way too nice to be part of an attack."

Drew grins. "You think I'm nice?"

Rosie blushes and turns away.

"I still think we should all be going," says Louisa, in her calm and peacekeeping way. "I mean, we've proven what a great team we are. And I'm going to be so worried about you two."

"We're going to be fine," I promise. "You guys just stay here and keep your fingers crossed."

The seven of us bunch together in a quick group hug, and then it's time for Alonso and me to go into our boxes.

"Watch out for Brianna," Louisa advises as she walks away.

As we climb into our individual boxes, I look at Alonso and I can tell he's nervous, too. According to the label on my box, I will be entering the new Phoenix facility impersonating a dozen cases of canned green beans. Alonso is posing as a year's supply of Cheezy-Wizard.

"Interesting," he says. "I've never thought of myself as resembling a can of Cheezy-Wizard before, but I'm willing to give it a try."

Around us, soldiers are climbing into boxes and oversized metal drum containers. A rush of pure pride fills me as I realize that all of this is happening because of me.

Then I duck into the darkness of the box as a Resistance soldier seals it up, leaving just enough room up top for me to breathe through.

Seconds later I feel a brawny soldier hoist me onto his shoulder and carry me up the truck's ramp with surprising ease.

While I wait for the engine to rev to life, I am aware of muffled whispers; through the heavy cardboard of my box, though, I can't tell what's being said. There is also some scuffling noise and the sound of dragging, along with a few grunts.

"Sparrow to Dictionary Dude," I say into my wristband communicator. "Come in, Dude."

"Dictionary Dude, present and accounted for." It's a huge relief to hear Alonso's familiar voice in the darkness.

"See you in the trenches," I say.

"Or the pantry," Alonso jokes nervously.

The ride from the Art Institute to the Phoenix School is short and without incident. Then we come to a stop. My stomach tightens. I hear the rear doors of the truck creak open, and then I'm swaying through space in the darkness of the box, riding on the capable shoulder of another undercover Resistance soldier. I can feel him climbing the stairs, then lowering me carefully to the ground. Through the cardboard, I hear other boxes being placed nearby.

Moments later, the truck is backing out of the loading zone.

Phase One of Operation Special Delivery has gone off without a hitch.

But this was the easy part.

Chapter 14

I pop out of my cardboard container like a life-sized jack-in-the-box.

When the three boxes closest to me all open at the same time, I nearly have a heart attack.

I find myself staring in shock at Louisa, Evelyn, and Rosie. The Cheezy-Wizard box containing Alonso is nowhere in sight.

I gasp, wide-eyed. "What did you guys do?"

"Right before the truck left," Louisa explains, looking a bit guilty, "we pushed Alonso's box down the ramp, away from the truck. Then we climbed into boxes ourselves."

"Do you guys have any idea how dangerous this is?" I demand in a whisper.

"Yes," says Evelyn. "In fact, I've calculated the number of faculty and, given their numeric proportion, the probability that they will notice four new kids is highly likely." She gives a brave nod. "But I'm okay with that."

"We've got your back," says Louisa, with a matter-of-fact shrug. "We're a team."

Rosie snorts. "I was just in the mood for a battle," she says, but I know she's here because she agrees with Louisa.

"It had to be the four of us!" says Evelyn. "That's how this all started, and that is how it's going to end."

Louisa gulps. "Please don't say 'end.'"

"You know what I mean," says Evelyn.

Since we don't have time to spare arguing, we creep through the pantry, where several larger boxes filled with soldiers will remain, awaiting our signal.

We make it through the empty kitchen easily enough.

Once we get out of the kitchen and into the halls, though, traffic picks up a bit.

The place is crazed. I suppose this is because the faculty is expecting the Resistance attack to happen sometime later today, and they're trying to get the students into their rooms and out of the way. This is a good thing for us. The Phoenix School is usually as organized and as regimented as it gets, which would make anyone or anything out of the ordinary (us, for example) stand out. None of us are in the standard-issue Phoenix dress of wearing our names on our jackets, which normally would get us singled out in ten seconds flat. But today this place is kind of a free-for-all. Kids are milling around and we merge into the stream of traffic, remembering to keep our eyes down.

I am nearly numb with dread. If anyone recognizes me — a student, a scout, a supervisor — I can't even begin to guess what they would do to me as punishment for my escape.

Occasionally, pairs of teachers wander past, checking off lists on their tablets and reminding one another about the specifics of their counterattack plan. As they pass, I hold my breath and lower my face. Each time, my skin gets a little clammier, my blood a little chillier. There is a faculty member posted at every first-floor window, waiting for the Resistance army's arrival. They bark orders to the students, but basically, they're too preoccupied to take notice of us four trespassers.

I hate how well I remember this place as I navigate confidently toward the Superior's office, which is on the third floor. When we come to a little-used stairwell, I turn in to it. This gives us some much-needed solitude.

Rosie shocks us all by announcing, "I'm going to find Ivan."

I whirl to face her. "No," I say firmly. "We should stay together."

Evelyn and Louisa agree with me, but Rosie won't budge. "Wren is heartsick," she explains. "She's so scared, not knowing if he's been hurt . . . or worse. I at least have to try!"

I sigh. I've been feeling the same way, not knowing what's become of Jonah. "You can't go alone," I say.

I'm surprised when Evelyn volunteers to join her. Despite what seemed to be a friendly truce between them earlier, they've been bickering again and disagreeing over everything. I point this out but Evelyn shakes her head.

"That's exactly why she needs me," says Evelyn reasonably. "We think differently. We'll see both sides of whatever situation we run into."

"She has a point," says Louisa.

"Okay," I say, nodding. "If they're holding Ivan, I'm guessing it's in the tunnel, you know . . . the one we used to escape."

"How could I forget?" says Rosie.

I make them promise that no matter what they find or don't find in that tunnel, they will go directly to the pantry when they hear the lockdown alarm. They agree, and are off.

Louisa and I watch them hurry down the stairs. Then we head up the next flight, taking the steps two at a time until we reach the third floor. I open the door quietly and peek out. I remember from my tour that very little goes on up here; Miss Castle, the Supervisor, likes things quiet when she's not teaching self-defense.

Confident that no one is around, we burst out of the stairwell onto the third floor. A quick sprint to our right takes us to the library meeting room that serves as the Superior's office.

This time it's Louisa who peeks in to see if anyone's lurking inside. She gives me a nod and we go in.

It's a pretty typical-looking office, with file cabinets and a laptop computer, and some phony teaching diplomas and credentials framed on the wall. On the desk sits a heavy-duty aluminum-sided briefcase. I can only imagine what Miss Castle keeps in there. Certainly not her knitting needles.

The far wall of the room is draped with a huge banner stretching from one side of the room to the other depicting the Phoenix Center emblem and motto. Seeing it makes me a little queasy.

"Where's the lockdown alarm?" asks Louisa, anxiously surveying the walls for a fire-alarm-type mechanism.

"I don't know exactly," I confess. "They just mentioned on the tour that this is where all school-wide commands originate. They didn't point out the location of the alarm."

"I guess they wouldn't," says Louisa.

We begin searching for levers, buttons, switches — anything that would be capable of sounding an alarm.

Then Louisa points at the big, glittering star hanging on the wall. It's a fancy rendition of the Alliance seal.

"It's worth a try," I whisper. I start to pull the star off the wall, and then I freeze. My breath catches in my throat. My eyes dart sideways and I strain my ears, listening.

"What's wrong?" asks Louisa.

I drop my hand. "I think you should go downstairs now . . . *right now* . . . and see if Evelyn and Rosie were able to find Ivan."

She looks at me like I've lost my mind. "And leave you here alone?"

"I'll be fine. I'll just check behind a few more things. Maybe it's not even in here."

208

"I don't know, Maddie," says Louisa, wringing her hands. "I think it's better if we stick to the plan. It's safer if we stay together."

Trust me, I'm thinking. *It's not.*

"I'll be fine," I assure her. "Go back to the pantry. I'll be there in two minutes, I promise." I hurry to remove my wristband device and thrust it at her. "Use this if you need it."

She looks at me for a long moment, and I'm afraid she's going to argue, but finally, she nods.

"Good luck," she says, just the way she did the day I took the training wheels off my bike.

The memory fills me and I nearly choke up. "You're my best friend," I blurt out.

"And you're mine," she whispers. "Always."

She disappears through the door and down the hall. And then there's that noise again. The rustling sound that made me freeze.

So I was right. I hadn't imagined it.

There *is* someone else in this office. Which is why I sent Louisa away. To protect her.

Now my hunch is further confirmed by the sound of the Phoenix banner being swept aside.

I turn to see Brianna standing there, pointing something at me. She is looking at me with those hateful eyes of hers and I can't help but feel a little sorry for her. What a horrible life she must have had to be so filled with anger and loathing. But this time, she doesn't shout threats at me; this time, she speaks in a ghostly whisper:

"I'm in trouble."

You and me both, I'm thinking, but I don't say it. I just continue to stare at the gadget she's holding, which is clearly some kind of remote control.

"I was sent here to be punished," she explains in her creepy, zombie voice. "I'm waiting for Miss Castle."

"Oh." My mouth is dry as I take a tentative step toward the door. "Well, then I'm sure you'll be wanting your privacy, so —"

"See that?" She motions with the remote to the aluminum briefcase on the desk. "That's something I made in pyrotechnics class. It's supposed to be my final project."

210

I swallow hard, guessing that the operative word in that sentence would be *final*.

"It's a bomb. A good one. A strong one. Better than any of these other pathetic cadets, or even the teachers, could have ever assembled. That's why Miss Castle got mad. She said I overstepped. She said I had no business making such a high-powered device. But I'll get even with her!" Brianna informs me.

"Um . . ." I hate to ask but I have to. "How exactly are you going to get even?"

"I'm going to blow up this place!"

She says this in such a delighted tone that it makes me shiver. I suppose I could try tackling her, but I'm afraid the action might set off the detonator she's holding.

Then she surprises me by asking a question. "What's it like?" she demands. "Tell me! What's it like?"

"What's *what* like?"

"Having friends. Having people who like you and won't betray you at any moment?"

She's got some nerve talking about betraying people, since she's the one about to blow up all of her classmates. But I decide not to point that out to her. She is looking away from me, her eyes suddenly wistful and sad. I take the opportunity to step the tiniest bit closer to her.

"You want to know what having friends is like?" I ask. "Well . . . I should tell you . . . it's actually pretty nice." I think of Louisa, Rosie, and Evelyn. I think of Alonso, Drew, and Ryan. And Jonah. I have to blink back the wetness in my eyes.

"I think I had friends once," she sighs, moving her index finger so that it is poised above a red-lit button on the detonator.

There is a scream in my throat but I don't let it out. "I'm sure you had great friends," I assure her, sneaking another step in her direction. "And you can have them again!" I take a deep breath and do my best to copy the soothing tone that Jonah used the day he saved me on the catwalk. "You're a smart girl, Brianna. You know this is a bad place. Let me help you get out of here, and I promise everything will be okay. Just don't press that button!"

Tears are spilling out of the corners of her eyes now, and the hand that holds the detonator is beginning to shake. She bites her lip, struggling with the decision. "I miss my friends."

"I'll be your friend," I whisper.

For a moment, she just stares and her expression is so blank I think she's forgotten I'm here. But then she blinks away a tear, and ever so slowly, she extends her hand — the one holding the detonator — in my direction.

Just as slowly, I reach out to meet it halfway. My fingers are about to close around it when I feel something powerful collide with me from behind.

The force is that of a freight train or a meteor.

The next thing I know, I've hit the floor.

And the detonator is gone.

Chapter 15

It wasn't a meteor or a freight train that took me down.

It was Miss Castle.

My kneecaps feel like they're shattered from the force with which they hit the floor, and my shoulder is throbbing where her birdlike body made impact with mine.

I am now certain that the rumor about Miss Castle killing a person with her pinkie finger is no rumor.

She studies me sprawled there on the floor — my short blond hair, the thick glasses — and frowns, puzzled as to who I am. But this disguise was only intended to work from a distance and it just takes her a minute to see through it.

"Well, if it isn't Madeleine Frye," Miss Castle says in a wicked singsong. "The one who got away."

I attempt to stand but she plants one scrawny foot on my already aching shoulder, pushing me back to the floor. I can see that she is now in possession of the detonator.

Her voice is shrill and her pale eyes are filled with fury. "The Alliance shall triumph! We and we alone will usher in the new order. The Alliance is the absolute power of the future, and I am a conduit of that power."

"No . . ." comes a strangled voice from behind her. Brianna lunges for her, but Castle dodges the attack, freeing me from where I was clamped beneath her foot. Fighting the pain in my knees and my shoulder, I struggle to my feet and hobble toward the Alliance star hanging on the wall. The lockdown alarm *has* to be behind it. It just has to.

"I knew you were trouble," Miss Castle snarls at Brianna, reaching for her. Brianna retaliates by lashing out with a strong kick and Miss Castle topples backward. The detonator skids across the carpet.

I reach the Alliance star and start tugging. It is affixed firmly to the wall.

Out of the corner of my eye, I see Miss Castle shake off her daze; she is slithering like a snake toward the detonator. . . .

At the last second, I manage to pry off the star. And then I'm staring at it: a lever. I flip it.

Suddenly, the building is filled with the earsplitting wail of the lockdown alarm. It pulses through the room, and into my already pounding head.

"The Alliance will triumph!" Miss Castle screams, and to my horror, she snatches up the detonator.

Brianna seems to move at light speed and in slow motion at the same time. She throws herself at Miss Castle.

But it's too late.

Miss Castle's finger is about to connect with the red button.

I race toward her, trip, and find myself flying.

"No!"

The scream that rips from my throat seems to drown out all sound — the stomping of Resistance boots as they storm into the room; the harsh metallic chorus of weapons preparing to fire; Miss Castle bleating about certain Alliance victories to come; Evelyn, Louisa, and Rosie calling my name, asking if I'm all right.

I hear nothing but my own voice, desperately roaring that word — *Nooooooo.*

And if there is an explosion, I don't hear that, either.

I don't feel the building shudder with the force of Brianna's bomb, and I don't smell the smoke or hear screams.

What I do feel is a sense of falling.

Then my forehead connects with the hard floor.

And the world goes black.

When I open my eyes, I don't know where I am.

I blink a few times to clear my vision and realize that I'm lying on a cot in the Phoenix School infirmary. This realization gets my heart pounding fast. I've got to get out! They'll drug me again, or worse. I've got to run, I've got to —

"Maddie. It's all right. You're safe."

I turn to see Dr. Ballinger sitting beside me. Her face seems to swim before my eyes. I attempt to sit up, but my head feels as though it's splitting in two.

"Easy," she says, gently guiding me back down to the cot. "No sudden movements just yet. You've got a pretty nasty bump. You fell when you were trying to stop the Superior."

What is she talking about? I close my eyes to let the aching subside. Then I force myself to remember: *soldiers in boxes, the lockdown alarm, Brianna, Miss Castle . . .*

The detonator!

This time I ignore the pain and sit bolt upright. "The bomb!" I cry.

"Maddie, relax," says Dr. Ballinger. "It's okay."

"But . . . but . . ." I stammer. "Brianna's bomb. I saw Miss Castle press the button."

"Yeah," comes Louisa's voice from across the infirmary. "Funny thing about that."

218

I turn my head — cautiously — to see her, along with Rosie and Evelyn, smiling at me.

"Miss Castle did hit a button. . . ." says Rosie. "But apparently, Brianna is as smart as she is spooky. She rigged the remote to require two separate but consecutive button sequences in order to detonate the bomb."

I actually manage to smile. "Another code."

"Yeah," says Evelyn. "I'm just glad that was one code nobody was able to crack."

"So our plan . . ." I begin, sitting up again, slowly. "Did it work? Did the soldiers capture the faculty in lockdown? Did they get the kids out?"

"It all went off like clockwork," says Rosie. "Thanks to you."

"And everyone's okay? No one got hurt?"

"The only injury is that bump on your head," says Louisa, walking over and slinging an arm around her mother. She's finally able to see her again, and this makes the pain even fainter. "Good thing we gave you bangs," Louisa adds with a small smile. "They'll cover it perfectly."

"And that's fortunate," says Evelyn with a sly grin, "because you're going to want to look your best."

"Huh?" I wonder if while I was unconscious they've all gone a little nuts.

Dr. Ballinger helps me off the cot. "Try not to let her get overly excited," she warns, and my friends laugh as they assist me out of the infirmary.

I don't know what they're laughing about until they guide me into the hallway. And then I see him, walking around the corner.

"Jonah!"

I rush over to him, not letting myself stop and think before I can give him a hug. I am so happy and relieved to see him that I forget all about the pain. "I was so worried about you!" I say.

He smiles, and I realize I've never seen him do that before. It's the best smile I've ever seen.

"I was fine," he assures me. "I'd been on the streets before. I knew where to hide, where to sleep for the night. And I knew I'd find you again." He studies me a moment, then smiles again, shyly. "Great haircut."

I blush. "Thanks."

Jonah explains how he was able to outrun the Alliance spies, but he didn't dare come back to Wrigley, in case any other spies had spotted him. "So I hid out near the Phoenix Center. I figured if you guys weren't able to decipher the flash drive, you might come back here to find Ivan."

"Ivan!" I gasp. "Is he all right? Did anyone find him?"

As if in answer to my question, a very happy Wren appears at the opposite end of the hallway. She's escorting Ivan, who's got some bruises and is limping slightly, but all in all, he seems okay.

"They had him locked up in the basement," Jonah explains.

When Wren and Ivan reach us, Ivan surprises me with a salute. "Nice work."

"Back at you," I say. "We couldn't have done it without your flash drive in the first place."

As Wren helps him to the infirmary, to be seen by Dr. Ballinger, I turn to my friends.

"Where's my mom?" I ask. "And what about Alonso,

Drew, and Ryan? Is Alonso mad that you guys pushed his box off the truck?"

"Nah, he's very forgiving," Evelyn says with a small smile.

"Follow us," says Louisa.

We go downstairs; the place is eerily quiet. Several soldiers are moving about, performing thorough checks of all the computers, collecting weapons, and seeing to other details. There are no zombie cadets in the halls now.

"The students all have been transported to the hospital," Evelyn explains. "They'll need to get the drugs out of their systems. Some have to be treated for burns from the boilers, but other than that, they're all going to be fine."

"What about the faculty?" I ask.

"They were *removed*," says Rosie, jerking her fingers into air quotes around that last word. "I don't know where they were taken or what's going to happen to them. I suppose I could ask, but I don't think I really want to know."

I shake my head. "Neither do I."

We find the boys in the lobby with my mother, who looks horrified at the sight of the bump on my head. Hornet or not, she's still my mom, and she makes a huge, embarrassing fuss over it.

"Does it hurt?" she asks, kissing it gently.

"Mom!" I protest. "I'm fine."

Louisa and Ryan exchange grins. Drew is looking at me as though he knows what I'm going through.

"Are you nauseous at all?" My mother is looking at me closely, her forehead wrinkled with concern. "Maybe you should ice that bump."

"Mom!" I sigh, exasperated. "Okay . . . I'll ice it, I'll ice it."

"Good." She nods, appeased. "All right, then, I'm just going to head down to the tunnel to confiscate the rest of the Taser wands and nerve gas canisters. Then we can go home and snuggle up on the sofa with some non-dairy Rocky Road. Oh, and your dad will be home tonight, too!" She kisses me again and marches off.

Rosie is pressing her lips together, trying not to giggle.

"Nerve gas and Rocky Road," notes Alonso. "Now, there's a combination you don't encounter every day."

"I think it's cute," says Evelyn, her eyes filled with longing. "I can't wait to see my mom."

"You don't have to!" says Ryan.

With that, the boys excitedly explain that my mother has already put people in charge of contacting everyone's families; their moms and dads are on the way here as we speak.

"We're going back home!" says Alonso.

At first, we all cheer, hugging one another from sheer joy. But then the reality sets in, and we get quiet. I sneak a look at Jonah, and my heart sinks, wondering where exactly he'll be going back to. Nobody speaks for a long moment.

Finally, I break the silence.

"It's going to be weird to be apart from you guys."

"Yeah," says Drew. "How am I gonna sleep tonight without Alonso snoring like a freight train in the next sleeping bag?"

"Wow." Louisa frowns. "So I guess we'll all be going back to our regular schools."

"Yeah, I guess so." Rosie drapes her arm around Evelyn's shoulders. "I'm going to miss being challenged by you every time I open my mouth," she teases.

I have a million things to say, but I can't seem to bring myself to say them. I think of Jonah, with nowhere to go, and of all the cadets who believed they were being rescued from a life in the street when the Alliance picked them up, posing as the benevolent Phoenix organization.

The sadness is nearly overwhelming.

But then I look around at the handsome old library lobby. My eyes go to the stairs, and I picture all that empty space on the upper floors. I remember the pantry stocked with healthy, non-drugged faculty food, and I think of Dizzy, with all the knowledge he has to share.

"Uh-oh," says Louisa, pointing at me, her eyes twinkling. "She's got that ironing-board look on her face again!"

She's right, of course. I do.

And suddenly, I'm smiling.

Chapter 16

L am back at the Phoenix Center.

Not as a prisoner this time, nor an undercover soldier.

But as a volunteer.

It's been weeks since the final showdown at the Phoenix Center. Between the data Ivan collected, and Evelyn's stolen documents, the Resistance has made great strides toward eliminating the Alliance presence in Chicago. I wish I could say the same for the rest of the country. There've been reports of mysterious fires and other kinds of destruction and sabotage from places all along the Canadian border. The Resistance is working as diligently as ever, but they've still got a long way to go.

We won a major battle here at the Phoenix Center. But there is still a war going on. It's important that we don't forget that.

It's also important that we don't forget what our country is fighting for, which is why Rosie, Evelyn, Louisa, and I are here at the former library today. My friends and I volunteered to reorganize the books the Alliance left behind. I'm so glad they weren't all burned in those awful boilers. I look forward to reading as many of them as I possibly can (even if it will be strange not to be reading them on my e-reader).

And thanks to the idea I had in the library lobby, there is a lot more to look forward to than that. This library is going to be turned into a school — the Harold Washington Academy — and it's going to include a military training program for any kids who are interested. The army is a part of all our lives, like it or not, and since we have no idea how long this War is going to last, we're going to need as many good soldiers as we can get. Dizzy, Wren, and Ivan are going to be teachers here, and most of the former Phoenix cadets are already enrolled as

227

students. Some were reunited with their families; others were old enough to enlist in the regular army. None of them — *none of them* — had to go back to the street.

As for us — Louisa, Alonso, Evelyn, Drew, and I are going to finish our regular schooling right here at the academy. Jonah, Ryan, and Rosie are also sticking around, but they've opted for military training. They've already signed up for special courses for officer candidates. Evelyn is also taking an accelerated military technology course.

Of course, we'll all have to enlist two years from now when we turn fifteen. Unless something changes, and the major conflicts are resolved.

Who knows? It could happen. That is what I hope for. What we all hope for.

My friends and I have been working here in the library for the last few days, and in the evenings, we ride out with my mom, searching the city for our friends — Helen, Troy, the Daggers. So far, we haven't found them. But I hope that if they ever need us, they'll know where we are.

Looking across the room now, I see Evelyn and Louisa whispering and I'm sure it has something to do with a big, important thing we've been planning for a while now.

Not a mission, or an escape, or an invasion.

Something totally normal. Something fun.

A slumber party.

It was Evelyn's idea, and the boys even joked about sneaking in through the window to crash the party. Then I reminded them my mother was the leader of the Resistance army, and they decided sneaking in probably wasn't the best idea.

We're going to get all the soychips and tofu ice cream we can get our hands on, and maybe we'll try giving Louisa a haircut this time, just to see how it turns out. But we haven't picked a date yet.

Now Wren calls to us that it's time to quit for the day. As we make our way down the stairs and through the main lobby of the library, Louisa says, "Okay. Evelyn and I were discussing when to have this slumber party. We need to get it on the calendar."

I nod, feeling determined. If we could help the Resistance infiltrate the Phoenix School and win a battle in the War, then we can certainly do *this*.

"Okay, so let's have it as soon as possible," I say, linking my arm through Louisa's. She links hers through Evelyn's, who links hers through Rosie's.

"How soon?" Louisa asks.

As we head for the doors, I smile. "Tomorrow, girls."

You never know
what will happen
tomorrow . . .

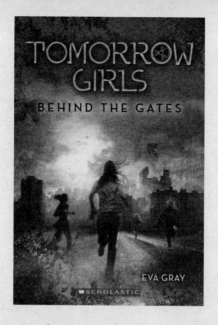

Tomorrow Girls #1: Behind the Gates

Disaster and destruction are all thirteen-year-old Louisa has ever known. But now she and her best friend, Maddie, are among the lucky few being sent to boarding school, far from home. Finally, a taste of freedom!

Country Manor School isn't perfect: The girls' roommates are tough to get along with, and the school is hard work. Still, Louisa loves CMS — the survival skills classes, the fresh air. She doesn't even miss not having TV, or the Internet, or any contact with home. It's for their own safety, after all.

Or is it?

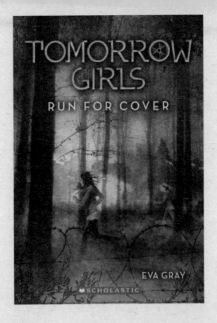

Tomorrow Girls #2: Run for Cover

Just when things have gotten kind of normal for Rosie, she finds herself running for her life — again. Only this time she's stuck with her roommates from school: Louisa, who can be okay sometimes; Maddie, who can't stop complaining; and Evelyn, the girl with a million conspiracy theories. If she weren't so scared, Rosie would be totally annoyed.

But one of Evelyn's theories was right: The boarding school the girls were sent to belongs to the Alliance, the wrong side of the War. Rosie has no choice but to run — and no one to rely on but her new friends. Whether she likes it or not.

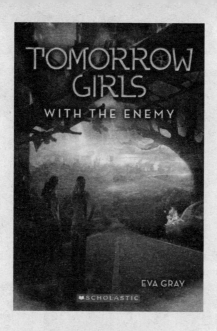

Tomorrow Girls #3: With the Enemy

Evelyn has always suspected that things are more sinister and more complicated than they seem. Now that Maddie has been kidnapped, Rosie, Louisa, and the boys are paying more attention to Evelyn's theories. As the group make their way toward war-torn Chicago, they're under constant threat of capture. Danger and dark surprises lurk around every twist of the road.

Evelyn knows they need a strategy to find Maddie. But what the group comes up with may be their riskiest plan yet: infiltrating the Alliance itself. Even Evelyn has her doubts. Can they save Maddie before it's too late?

POISON APPLE BOOKS

The Dead End

This Totally Bites!

Miss Fortune

Now You See Me...

Midnight Howl

Her Evil Twin

Curiosity Killed the Cat

At First Bite

THRILLING.
BONE-CHILLING.
THESE BOOKS
HAVE BITE!